PRAISE F

MW01486898

"Best-selling author Leslie Wolfe weaves a first-class collection of 19 suspense stories with intriguing twists and turns that will easily captivate the reader from the first page to the last. "

"This was a fascinating and captivating read that had me immersed from the beginning."

"The book is expertly crafted and each section is full of wonderful stories."

"his is a collection of short stories that will hit you right in your heart. They are all emotionally charged, all different but linked by extreme feelings and conflict."

"Enjoyed each story! Each one had a plot that wouldn't let you stop until you finished the story."

"A great collection of short stories. Each story had a theme of either Love, Lies, or Murder. Three wonderful groups of stories."

PRAISE FOR LESLIE WOLFE

"I do love Leslie Wolfe's stories and novels and very much look forward to each of them."

"Leslie Wolfe is one of my favorite authors. She sends out occasional free short stories in her newsletters, so when I saw this book I jumped at it. "

"I have read every novel Leslie Wolfe has written and anxiously await for a new one to follow. She is without a doubt, one of my favorite authors."

LOVE, LIES
AND MURDER

BOOKS BY LESLIE WOLFE

TESS WINNETT SERIES

Dawn Girl
The Watson Girl
Glimpse of Death
Taker of Lives
Not Really Dead
Girl with A Rose
Mile High Death
The Girl They Took

DETECTIVE KAY SHARP SERIES

The Girl From Silent Lake
Beneath Blackwater River
The Angel Creek Girls

BAXTER & HOLT SERIES

Las Vegas Girl
Casino Girl
Las Vegas Crime

STANDALONE TITLES

Stories Untold
Love, Lies and Murder

ALEX HOFFMANN SERIES

Executive
Devil's Move
The Backup Asset
The Ghost Pattern
Operation Sunset

For the complete list of Leslie Wolfe's novels, visit:
LeslieWolfe.com/books

LOVE, LIES AND MURDER

LESLIE WOLFE

II **ITALICS**

Italics Publishing

$\varint$ **ITALICS**

Italics Publishing Inc.
Edited by Joni Wilson and Susan Barnes.
Cover and interior design by Sam Roman.
ISBN: 978-1-945302-88-6

LOVE

THE BANJO

He ran parallel with the train as fast as he could, reaching for the handlebar and trying to figure out how he could hop inside, when the freight car was that high. It was above his waist level, and he needed to grab onto something with both his hands and pull himself inside the car, if he didn't want the risk of slipping under the car and losing one or both of his legs in the process.

Freight train hopping was more difficult than he'd expected. He was almost out of breath and the train seemed to move faster, catching speed, while the distance between his extended hand and the handle he was aiming for increased inch by inch. At least that car had its door wide open and seemed empty. If he could only push forward some more, gain up on the damn thing, come close enough to venture a foot up that step, while grabbing onto the handle.

The train squealed and slowed down, as the tracks curved a little, and he pushed himself to run faster. Then he lunged forward with the last drop of energy he had left, and grabbed that handle while his left foot found the wide step underneath the car's open door. His right arm flailed in the air, desperately looking for something to grab, while his body was pushed backward by inertia. Then he felt a strong hand grip his right wrist and yank him up forcefully. He landed face down on the car's floor, while the same strong grip dragged him all the way inside.

"A thing like that could get you killed out here," he heard a man's voice say calmly.

He looked up at the man who'd pulled him inside. He was young, barely twenty years old, if even. His face was grimy, smudged with dust and sweat and dirt, and his clothes were nothing unexpected for a habitual train hopper. His blue eyes were fixed on his Rolex, and he quickly covered it with the sleeve of his windbreaker.

Still panting hard, he pulled himself up to his feet and shook the young man's hand.

"Thanks," he said, "I appreciate it."

"Huh," the young man replied with a grin, dazzling white teeth sparkling against the grime on his face. "You should." Then he laughed, a quick laugh cut short by a few coughs. "You're no train-hopper material, dude," he continued when he was able to catch his breath. "What, you got lost, or somethin'?"

"Nah," he replied, still panting. "Just looking for someone."

The young man whistled. "So, you got a place to live, and nice clothes, and food, but you hop trains for fun?"

"Not for fun, no. I'm looking for my brother," he replied. "Someone said he might have been riding freight trains through these parts of the country."

The young man gave him a good look, head to toe, and he felt he was being evaluated. Maybe the kid was thinking how much money he had on him, or if it was worth killing him. He held his gaze steadily, unafraid, glad to feel the holster of his weapon tight against his ribs.

"Name's Travis," the kid said, extending his dirty hand again.

He took it and shook it firmly. "Jack."

"Got some food on you, Jack?"

He hesitated a split second, then took out two of the chocolate bars he'd stuffed his pockets with before leaving the city.

Travis took one carefully, almost as if he expected him to slap him or punch him or something. Then he whistled again, and slowly unwrapped the bar, savoring the experience. Then he wolfed it down in two good bites, chewed hastily with his mouth open.

"Umm, good stuff."

Jack watched him eat and felt something tug at his heart. This kid was about the same age as Conrad, his younger brother who had vanished almost two months ago. Conrad was going home from school one day, and it was later than usual. He'd stayed at school longer, working in the lab with three other med-school students, colleagues of his at Northwestern University Feinberg School of Medicine, and those three students were the last people to have seen him.

From the lab, he had to cross the campus and walk a few blocks through Streeterville, to the Brown Line train station. From what Jack was able to deduce, it was already dark when Conrad had left the university about seven, his banjo strapped on his back, and a small backpack in his hand. That's the way his colleagues described his appearance that day. He was his normal self, maybe a little tired after a long day studying countless blood samples on the electronic microscope, and he'd told everyone he was hungry.

Then he vanished. When he didn't come home that night, Jack had called the cops, but Conrad was an adult and they weren't going to open an investigation for at least twenty-four hours. His brother's phone was going straight to voicemail and, lacking any other means of investigating, Jack had gone to the university the next morning. He talked with Conrad's colleagues and heard that he had been in a good mood the day before, doing his usual routine after lunch, when he sang a couple of songs in front of the building for his cheering colleagues and passersby. There was no girlfriend who anyone knew about, nor did he seem disturbed by anything. He'd just left the night before, going home, as he normally did.

Only he'd never made it home.

Jack retraced his steps, with the help of a couple of students who'd walked to the Chicago/Franklin Brown Line with Conrad before, and knew which side of the street he liked to walk on, and where he usually stopped for a snack before hitting the train station. He walked the same street, by the ballpark, carefully observing every detail, yet almost missed the white wood shards that littered the street corner, next to some tangled, coiled banjo strings.

When he realized what those were, all the blood rushed to his chest and his heart thumped heavily, as if fighting to escape his chest cavity. He dropped to his knees next to the scattered pieces of wood, and took one in his hand, gently running his fingers over the glossy finish. Then he crouched lower, looking under the nearby trash can and saw a photo, barely showing from underneath some street litter. He grabbed it with two fingers and held his breath. He already knew what it was, an old photo of Conrad and him, when they were much younger, taken the day Jack had bought Conrad the banjo.

That day Jack had taught him how to play it, and Conrad, a talented guitarist and a natural for anything with strings, was playing the theme song from *Doctor Zhivago* before the end of the day. Not perfectly, but it was recognizable, and soon thereafter it was better, the twangy sound of the banjo warm and full under his fingers, sounding more and more like the balalaika in the original theme song. Since that day, Conrad had kept their picture tucked inside his instrument's pot, taped in place with a piece of transparent adhesive tape still clinging to the photo in Jack's hand.

He moaned loudly when he noticed the bloodstain on the photo, and, as if living through a nightmare, he heard one of Conrad's colleagues make a 911 call.

Nothing happened after the cops came; nothing useful anyway. Yeah, they'd confirmed the blood on the photo was his brother's. But that's where the trail went cold, despite countless video cameras scattered in the area, and endless interviews with pedestrians whose normal commute took them along the same street at about the same time of day. Then they speculated Conrad might be dead, a John Doe in some morgue, or an amnesic lost somewhere in the hospital system. But they couldn't find him anywhere, not in any morgue or hospital.

Jack didn't trust the police would do a good enough job. Per their official statement, they didn't have anything to go on. No other evidence, no body, no witnesses. Instead, they had countless crimes happening in Chicago every day, so many they were overwhelmed with work and unable to continue pursuing a case that had gone cold that quickly. But Jack didn't give up. He took the rest of the semester off, leaving his students in the capable hands of a colleague, and took to the streets, determined to find out what happened to Conrad. He talked to people, and spent day after day at that street corner, with Conrad's photo in his hands, showing it to everyone.

He was about to give up, defeated, although he still dreamed at night that his brother was out there somewhere, waiting for him, needing his help. But he'd already spoken with everyone, and he recognized almost all the people who commuted on that street on a daily basis. He kept going to that street corner though, as he'd done every day for the past month, and showed Conrad's photo to anyone willing to take a look. More and more people threw sympathetic, sad glances his way, while slowly shaking their heads; no, they hadn't seen him. Not then, not since.

Until one day, he found a homeless woman at that street corner, going through the trash can with shaky fingers. She stared at the photo for a long time, then said she must have been mistaken, because the man she'd seen still had his banjo. It was banged up, but the man still played, mostly at night, riding the freight trains. She'd seen him on the Burlington

Northern Santa Fe rail, headed south, like many others, fleeing the cold and bitter wind of Chicago winters. Or maybe it was Union Pacific? She didn't remember. Probably he was going to California, but she wasn't sure; the man she'd seen didn't talk. He just played sad songs, she'd added, some reminding her of movies she'd seen, many years ago when she still was somebody who had a life.

Now, looking at that kid munching on the second chocolate bar, he only hoped that someone out there had shared their food with Conrad, wherever he was.

"So, who you're looking for?" Travis asked, wiping his mouth with an off-brown sleeve.

Jack took out Conrad's photo. "This is my brother; his name is Conrad. He disappeared from Chicago, two months ago. Have you seen him?"

Travis smacked his lips and sucked his teeth. "What if he don't wanna get found, huh? Man's got the right to roam free, ya know."

"If I find him and he tells me to get lost, I will," Jack said. "Have you seen him?"

Travis thought for a while, biting his lower lip. "I should be smarter than this and milk you of some cash, but you're an okay guy. No, I haven't seen him, but train beaters barb about some guy playing a banjo on them trains."

"Where? When?" Jack asked, suddenly invigorated.

"On the UP lines, mostly, back and forth from California. It's like the man doesn't wanna get anywhere; just wants to ride. Maybe he's a gypsy, not like you and me. But that's just what I heard tramps talk, that's all. I haven't seen him."

"What the hell is a UP line?" Jack asked, frowning impatiently.

"Union Pacific, man. You gotta learn your trains if you want a future that don't end up in the big house."

Jack scrambled to the car's open door, looking outside as if getting ready to jump off the train.

"Whoa, hold it; you're on a UP train now. Relax."

He still stared into the darkness of the moonless night, letting the wind cool off his burning face. One second his heart swelled with hope, and then next it dropped to the abyss of despair. How was he going to find Conrad among so many trains, going in all directions? He could spend years searching and not find him, passing him in the night without even knowing.

Then he turned toward Travis, a glimmer of renewed hope glinting in his eyes. "Will you help me? I got money. I got more in the bank. I just want to find him."

Travis stared at him for a long moment, then muttered, "Uh-huh, it's not like I got any prior engagements, if you know what I mean," he laughed, then coughed some more. "Get some sleep. We'll need to change trains, hit the California line."

Jack sat on the dirty floor, leaning against the car's rusty wall, and tried to doze off but couldn't. The train was going faster, rattling and chugging rhythmically against the tracks. Then it slowed and pulled into a side line where it stopped with a long, screeching sound of iron against iron.

"Uh-oh," Travis said, jumping to his feet. "Not good. Bulls might come."

"Say what?"

Travis rolled his eyes. "Bulls, as in railroad cops. They catch us here, we're screwed." He leaned outside, checking the surroundings. It was quiet and dark, nothing moved.

"Ah, we're cool," he said, "we're on a branch line. They're keeping us parked here until another train passes us by. We're low priority," he scoffed, "we're unimportant. What else is new?"

Then he curled on the floor, hands folded under his head in a makeshift pillow. "Great time to nap," he muttered, half-asleep. "It's quiet for a bloody change."

He followed suit, but only leaned against the car wall as he'd done before; he couldn't bring himself to put his face on that grungy floor. The long hours caught up with him, because he dozed off without even knowing it. He dreamed of his brother, playing the banjo, and sometimes singing with it, although he always thought his voice didn't reach the skill of his fingers. But whenever music transported him, he added words and vocals to the instrument, and Jack loved the end result, although Conrad didn't always. Then the sound of a chugging train overlapped, almost drowning the banjo chords, and his eyes opened wide. He lunged to the door and held his breath.

There it was, faint, disappearing with the passing train, the sound of a banjo in the darkness. Without thinking, he got off the train and started running to catch the other one, his feet unstable against the loose ballast. He didn't care, and he forged ahead, clinging to the sound of that banjo as if it were a lifeline. Then he heard Travis behind him, coming fast.

"Move it, if you wanna catch this one, it's a dicer! Move your ass!" he yelled, and slapped his back as he passed him. He was younger, taller, faster, all helpful traits with train hopping.

Travis got his footing on a car and pulled himself inside, then yanked his arm and Jack let himself be pulled up, flailing desperately until he landed on the dirty floor of a freight car covered in loose straw that stunk of cow dung. But he didn't care; if he listened hard enough, somewhere under the chugging noise of the train, he could still hear the sound of the banjo.

"How do we get to him?" he asked, as soon as he could catch his breath.

"Ever been on a train car before?" Travis asked. "On top of it?" he added, gesturing with his finger.

He shook his head.

"It ain't that hard, I'll teach you," Travis said. "Let's wait until we clear the branch line. Someone might see us."

Jack looked at the kid with unspoken gratitude. He could've robbed him by now, taken his money, his cards, and his watch, or just killed him altogether. Instead, the kid was helping him, without asking for anything in return.

"What's your story?" Jack asked. "How come you're here?"

Travis smiled crookedly and turned away a little. "It was either this, or the system. My mom died, and they came to get me. My foster family was crooks, really bad people. I couldn't stay."

"How old are you?" Jack asked.

"Almost eighteen," Travis replied. "Soon I'll be able to do something other than ride these trains. Don't know what, and don't know how, but at least they won't chase me no more."

Slack-jawed, Jack found himself at a loss for words. He worked with young people, he was used to seeing them in school, clean and fed and loaded with attitude, texting and laughing and undisciplined. He wasn't prepared to see someone so young battle life on his own like that, starving on a train.

"Let's get going, we're good now," Travis said. "This cannonball's slowed down a little."

He led the way, demonstrating skill and athletic dexterity in getting them to the end of the car, then on top of the next car. From there, knees shaking worse than they'd ever done, Jack crawled on all fours behind the daring, young boy, who walked the train upright, wind in his face, unafraid as only teenagers can be.

As they got closer to the engine, the sound of the banjo grew louder, clearer, and Jack started to recognize some of the songs his brother used to play. Energized, he felt his fear vanish, and came down from the car's rooftop like a pro, imitating all of Travis' moves without hesitation. Then Travis pulled open a panel, and they entered the car where the banjo sounds were coming from.

It was dark, and the open side door only let occasional, distant light come in. The man didn't stop playing when they entered, and didn't look at them. He continued to play, his fingers comfortable and accomplished on the strings. Jack approached him, holding his breath.

"Conrad?" he called, but the man didn't stop playing.

He stared at the man and didn't recognize his brother. It was dark, and the man wore an unkempt beard that could have been growing for about two months. His clothes were so grimy, he couldn't tell if they were the ones Conrad had last been seen wearing. Jack resigned to listen, crouched on the floor next to the man, not daring to breathe. Soon a new day would break, and he'd know.

When the early light broke through the panels of the freight car, the man laid his banjo on the floor and closed his eyes. Jack searched the man's face, looking for a familiar trait, and couldn't be sure.

"Conrad," he called again, quietly. "It's me, Jack," he said, touching the man's arm.

The man kept his eyes closed, as if sleeping.

"May I?" Jack asked, gesturing toward the banjo, but the man didn't say anything and didn't open his eyes.

He took the banjo gently and started playing "Lara's Song," the theme music from *Doctor Zhivago.* In his hand, it sounded weird, almost unrecognizable; he'd never had Conrad's talent, only schooling. Note after note, the music came back to him, and his playing became stronger, more confident, and more recognizable.

When he started playing the unmistakable chorus, the man's eyes opened, and in those green irises Jack recognized his brother. He smiled and continued playing, hoping Conrad would say something, but he remained quiet. He watched Jack play the entire song, his eyes speaking volumes, but his words absent.

Then Jack set the banjo down and took out the photo. Conrad looked at it without a sound, but after a while, he took it and tucked it inside his banjo.

"Yes, yes," Jack exclaimed, "that's us, Conrad. You and me." Whatever had happened to his brother, there was still a part of him left intact, buried deep inside that man, and that part would guide Conrad home, just as it had helped him find another banjo to replace the broken one.

The train screeched and stopped, and Travis quickly pulled the door shut. "Trouble," he said. "Be quiet. We're in a big station; I believe it's Yuma."

"Good," Jack replied, and helped his brother to his feet. "We're going home. Come on, Conrad, let's go."

He pulled the car door open and jumped off, then Travis handed him the banjo and helped Conrad down. The kid's eyes were hollow, and his lower lip trembled a little. Jack took his hand to his pocket, and then changed his mind.

"You too, kid."

Travis stood there, in the doorway, staring, stunned.

"Yeah, you're coming home with us. Come on, it will be fun to have another brother. We might even teach you how to play the banjo."

A REASON

He lay immobile on the hospital bed, listening to the sounds around him. Faint street hubbub and car horns coming from outside. Distant hospital clamor, muffled by the closed door. The occasional PA system announcement, sometimes coded, sometimes not. He wondered what "code blue" meant. Was that the code associated with someone having a cardiac arrest? Turning blue? Do people actually turn blue when their heart stops, or was that just a myth?

The faint beeping of his heart monitor was boringly steady. No chance of a code blue in his room, no matter how hard he wished for it. There was a ringing in his right ear, and his right arm felt incredibly weak and heavy, like it had turned to stone. He tried to move it, but soon gave up, after achieving but a tiny movement in the finger wearing the oximeter.

His vision was blurry, but he realized he could see better if he closed his right eye. Still, the images refused to enter full focus; not that it mattered, though, considering he had nothing to look at, other than white ceiling tiles, and a muted TV someone had forgotten and left tuned to the shopping channel. Lacking interest in everything, he closed his eyes and let himself slip back into deep sleep.

"Hello, I'm Dr. Carrell," a young voice said, waking him.

He blinked a few times, until the figure of the man standing beside his bed came into relative focus.

"I'll be your attending, Mr. Pearce," the man continued, with a slight hesitation and frown when he said his name. "You've had a hemorrhagic stroke," the man continued, his voice infused with more kindness than before. "It's all good;

we've stopped the bleeding inside your brain and relieved the pressure."

He tried to speak, but his parched throat refused to make a sound. He swallowed hard, then tried again.

"Let... me... die," he whispered, then let a long, raspy breath of air escape his lungs.

The doctor frowned again and marked something on his chart.

"No need for that," he said gently. "You have a slight hemiparesis, a side effect from the stroke. Not to worry, we'll get you better with physiotherapy."

The doctor smiled patiently. He was young, so unbelievably young.

He closed his eyes again, chasing away unwanted shadows, memories of a distant past, of a time when everything seemed possible.

"Mr. Pearce? Is there someone we could call?"

A tear rolled from his left eye and got lost somewhere in his head bandage.

"Let... me... die," he repeated, a little louder this time. He drilled his blurry vision into the man's eyes. "Please."

The doctor pulled a chair closer to the bed and sat on it, abandoning the chart on the night stand.

"All right... But before we go there, let me share with you a story, something that happened to me when I was a young boy."

The doctor paused for a second, waiting for him to reply. He just nodded a little, or maybe he didn't, really.

"It was Thanksgiving Day, and my mother was driving us, my older brother and me, home from the market. She worked two jobs, my mom, and she didn't have time to get a turkey and everything else until that morning. She was a little cranky, I remember it clearly, because I kept banging my feet against her seat, and she kept yelling at me to stop. I didn't," he clarified, letting a sad smile appear on his lips. "The rain began as soon as we loaded the car. We started our way back home in a heavy downpour, cold as hell, darkening the early evening to almost pitch black."

He stopped his recount for a short while, staring into emptiness.

"We lived outside the city back then. It was only what a blue-collar, single mom with two kids could afford, you see. We had a long drive ahead of us, some thirty miles of dark, winding road, cutting through a forest. A few miles into that drive, our car broke down. It sputtered a few times, choked, then finally died, right there, in the middle of the road. Mom cursed at first, but then started crying and slamming her hand into the steering wheel. After a while, we all got out in the rain and pushed the car to the side of the road. She kept the four-way blinkers on, for safety. Then she continued to cry, quietly, ignoring our questions. 'What are we going to do, Mom?' we kept asking, but she had no answer to give."

Dr. Carrell stopped talking and swallowed a couple of times, trying to keep the mist away from his eyes.

"A stranger came out of nowhere, banged on her window, and scared all of us. We yelled, us boys, but she rolled down the window a crack and heard the man ask her what was wrong. He stood there, in the rain, and tried to get her engine to start. It didn't, but he wouldn't give up. He pulled out a mobile phone and called someone. Then he told us he was going to take care of things."

He smiled, the kind smile reserved for cherished memories.

"You see, my mom was scared of him at first. What if he was going to hurt us? You never know with strangers, in the middle of the night, in that forest. Then the tow truck showed up and she seemed relieved. She watched the driver hook up her car, then she told us boys to climb into the tow truck. Before we could do that, the stranger smiled and invited us all to his home, for Thanksgiving dinner. I remember my mother frowning, worried, unsure what to do."

The young man stopped talking again and checked on his patient. Vitals were good.

He kept on listening; he hadn't fallen asleep.

"I remember his house. It was huge, at least compared to what we were used to. He had this big dog, Shep was his name. Back then I didn't know, but today I can tell you it was a Newfoundland dog. The man lived alone in that house, but someone had prepared a full Thanksgiving dinner and set the table for one, leaving the turkey in the oven, to keep warm.

"He didn't speak much, the stranger. Without many words, he got us all clean, dry clothes that didn't really fit, and had started a fire in the massive fireplace. It crackled loudly, and Shep lay down in front of it, his head resting on his paws while he watched us eat. Not many words were spoken at that table. We, the kids, were intimidated by him, and we could barely eat at first; eventually hunger took over and we gulped everything down like there was no tomorrow. Mom was uncomfortable and kept her eyes lowered, unsure what to say. The man's home seemed gloomy, despite the happy fire and the loving dog; later we learned he had lost his wife and child in a terrible accident, earlier that same year."

The doctor repressed a sigh, watching another tear roll down his patient's cheek.

"After we'd eaten everything, including slices of excellent pumpkin pie, the man turned on the TV and sat in an armchair, inviting us with a gesture to make ourselves at home. Mom wanted to leave and asked to call a cab, but he said simply, 'There will be a time for that. Now you can rest.' She took a seat in another armchair, while us kids crawled on the thick carpet and played with Shep."

He smiled again, the same crooked, kind smile reserved for special moments in time.

"She fell asleep, right there, in that stranger's armchair," he continued, his voice catching a little. "You see, it was the first time in many months my mother felt she could rest for a while. We weren't hungry or cold anymore. She slept for hours, without moving, while the stranger watched over her, and hushed us whenever our play got too rowdy. Soon enough, though, we'd fallen asleep ourselves on the thick carpet, curled up with a large, black dog, in front of the fireplace that he kept going the whole night.

"The next morning, Mom startled out of her sleep and jumped to her feet, embarrassed beyond telling. He appeased her, then told her the car would be done in another day or so and taken to an address of her choosing. No, she didn't owe him anything, except a promise. She was supposed to always take her car for oil changes at that same service shop. He called us a cab, and we were gone, whispering many thanks and averting our eyes. You see, we didn't know how to react to that type of kindness. It wasn't like we'd seen kindness many times before.

"Mom kept her promise and always took our car to that same shop. They were slow to service it, you know. Sometimes an oil change took a full day, but that car never broke down again. My guess was the mechanics repaired everything that was wrong with it, every time, and kept it going. She always paid $19.99, not a dime more... they kept saying it was a coupon price, or something like that. But she wasn't stupid; she knew it was him, the man we'd met on Thanksgiving Day. A few years later, after she took the car in for yet another oil change, the shop manager apologized profusely. Apparently, one of the employees had totaled it while test driving it, and, as compensation, they offered her a brand-new Honda Civic."

He wiped the corner of his eye, discreetly, after making sure no one saw him from the hallway. Then he stood slowly and grabbed the chart off the table.

"You might not know what that meant, Mr. Pearce. That old car continuing to run, and the one after it, meant my mother could keep her job and keep us in school. That car meant my brother and I got to go to college, instead of joining gangs and going to prison. It meant that someone showed us the power of kindness and forever altered the course of our lives. Yes, I'm up to my tonsils in medical school debt, but I have a life, and so do my brother and my mother."

He opened his eyes and looked at that young doctor's face. His vision, still blurry, didn't cooperate much, and soon he gave up, closing his eyes again.

"You might wonder what that means, huh? That means you have to go to physio, because Lark, your Newfoundland dog, is in a kennel, waiting for you to take him home. It's a note here, in your chart. One of the EMTs took care of him."

The man opened his eyes again, then closed his right eyelid and focused a little better.

"I guess Shep's gone, huh?" the doctor asked softly. "He must have gotten old."

Mr. Pearce nodded once, just slightly.

Dr. Carrell clutched the chart under his arm, getting ready to leave. He grabbed the door handle and let his smile widen somewhat.

"So get your rear in gear, old man," he said in a cheerful tone, "because you're not done yet, and you're not that old either. There's plenty more kindness needed on the face of this earth. You've got work to do."

He lay immobile on the hospital bed, listening to the faint sounds surrounding him. A child crying somewhere, maybe on a different floor. Traffic outside, rushing in all directions. The occasional PA system announcement, coded or not. The beeping sound of his heart monitor, steady as they come. Strong and steady.

At the first light of dawn, he summoned all his willpower and unhooked himself from the monitors, then pulled the IV needle from his vein. With humongous effort, he willed his inert limbs to obey and leaned on the side of his bed, wobbly, ignoring his growing nausea. He somehow managed to get off the bed, leaning on his strong arm, and supporting most of his weight on his left foot. Slowly, shuffling more than walking, and using any object in his path for support, he made it to the doorway and stopped, too weak to let go of the door handle.

An orderly walked by and rushed toward him when he saw him struggle.

"Let's get you back to bed," he said, grabbing his elbow.

He pulled his elbow out of his grasp, and gave him a fierce, albeit unfocused glare.

"Where's that damn physiotherapy department?"

TOUR OF DUTY

It was the wrong time and place to enjoy anything, crossing an endless stretch of dusty, barren desert, leaving Kandahar and heading toward Panjwai, to check out a location rumored to be a new ISIL foothold. No, it wasn't the time to appreciate the sunrise, or the purple hues of the early morning sky, seen through the dust raised by the lead Humvee. Yet, he found himself barely containing a smile.

Hulk whimpered quietly and he turned his head and locked eyes with him. He seemed agitated, but continued to sit in the cargo area, wearing his full TEDD gear. That's what Hulk was, a TEDD, or tactical explosive detection dog. A combat K9 unit. A lifesaver.

He hushed him with a gesture, but his emerging smile had vanished, together with the enjoyment of the early morning sunrise. He tightened the grip on his M16 rifle, and frowned. The Humvee in front of them had slowed a little, and the road had turned bumpier.

"Doodley, your mutt stinks, man," Private Adams commented. He rode right behind him, and he hated dogs. What kind of man hates dogs? Probably some lame-ass pussy, that's who.

"Your mother stinks too, Adams," he replied dryly, then shot his dog another look and his frown deepened, as soon as he noticed Hulk's shift in attitude. His ears had perked up, and his nostrils flared, while he whimpered and became agitated, circling in the small confinement of the Humvee cargo area. He looked behind and saw the third Humvee in the convoy falling a few yards behind. He didn't like that, any of it. He decided to say something about it.

"Corporal, sir, we need to s—"

An explosion ripped through the air, sending the lead Humvee into shards, quickly engulfed in a ball of fire. He heard himself scream, faintly, and felt the air leave his lungs, but soon all he could hear was a high-pitched ringing in his ears. He knew he was screaming, only didn't know the reason, and didn't understand why he couldn't hear any of it. He gasped for air, as if drowning in a sea of pain and confusion, and slowly, the dust and smoke cleared.

The first thing he heard was Hulk's howls. Then he heard himself scream again, the moment he saw the bloodied, mangled iron that stood where his right leg used to be. He flailed and tried to reach out, to touch his leg, to make sure it was still there, but couldn't. Strong arms took him away from the Humvee and set him down on the ground.

"Put a lid on it, Marine," his corporal said, "help's on the way."

Hulk's incessant howls almost covered the distant radio garbles. He grabbed the corporal's pant leg.

"Hulk?" he asked, between heavy, shuddering breaths.

"He's all right, Marine."

"He's... hurt?"

The corporal yanked his pant loose from his grip. "Told you, Dood, he's fine. He's right there, see for yourself."

He made an effort to raise his head off the ground and saw Hulk, held tightly on a leash by another one of the guys, a new recruit. Hulk still howled, ears held back and tight against his skull, looking at him, sniffing the air heavy with the stink of blood and smoke and burned flesh.

Someone fussed over his wound, and soon an unbearable pain ran through his leg all the way to his chest, suffocating him. He fought, trying to free himself, but someone kept him still. Then everything faded into blackness.

He dreamed he was back at base, sleeping, with Hulk's strong spine tucked against him. They'd been sleeping like that since the day they'd assigned Hulk to him, and they started drills together. He wanted the dog by his side at all times, but regulations didn't allow dogs to enter sleep quarters. Therefore, he ended up trading the bunk for a hard stretch of the concrete kennel floor.

They'd grown inseparable quickly, and Private First Class, K9 Unit Handler Sean Doodley took all the jokes without flinching. Yes, he was spooning the dog. Yes, he liked to sleep in dog piss. Yes, dog hair was the new standard issue uniform. So what? Let them jawbone ahead, air is cheap and talk is less. What the two of them had together, none of these sorry losers did, or understood, for that matter. They were survivors; the two of them, and they were good at their job. The best tactical explosive detection unit the Marine Corps had ever seen.

As for Hulk, a three-year-old Malinois, he followed Doodley everywhere he went, and didn't take his eyes off him for one second. They worked together well, and Hulk had an impeccable success rate. On countless times he'd sniffed out IEDs way before they could hurt the unit. Probably that day would have been no different, if he'd paid closer attention to Hulk's signals. In his dream, he lost touch of Hulk; he was no longer there. He panicked.

He woke up screaming, and immediately a nurse rushed to his bedside and injected a syringe filled with clear liquid into his IV.

"Hello, Marine, and welcome to the R3MMU," the young nurse said, keeping a pair of concerned blue eyes riveted on him.

"Where... where am I?" he whispered, licking his chapped lips and trying to focus his eyes. All he saw was white—white walls, ceiling, and windows.

"The R3MMU," she repeated, "at Kandahar Airfield. Role 3 Multinational Medical Unit," she added, seeing how confused he was. "The hospital."

"What... happened?"

"An IED, says here," she replied quietly, tapping on his medical chart with a thin, long finger. "You're among the lucky ones. You made it out alive. You'll rotate home in about a week or so."

"Hulk?" he asked, his eyes filled with panic. "Where is he?"

The nurse checked the chart briefly. "Is that one of your buddies? I'm sorry; I don't know who that is. Why don't you get some rest? The doctor will be here soon."

That's how it all started. For most wounded warriors, losing a leg is a ticket home. For Doodley, it was a one-way ticket to hell, because leaving Hulk behind was nothing short of that.

He fought to stay deployed with every shred of willpower he could muster. He pleaded with his corporal and with the staff sergeant, but they both said the same things: regulations didn't allow an amputee to reenlist without being fitted with a prosthetic; he had to complete the rehabilitation program in the Warrior Transition Unit; and being reassessed from a physical and psychological fitness perspective was mandatory. Even so, returning to active duty for him most likely would mean serving in the National Guard somewhere. After all, Kandahar is not exactly compliant with the Americans with Disabilities Act.

As soon as he could leave the hospital bed, he took his first wheelchair trip, to see his staff sergeant one more time, at Kandahar International Airport, right across the airfield from R3MMU. It was his last chance. The staff sergeant gave him exactly two minutes.

"PFC Doodley, right? What do you need, son?"

"Hulk, sir. They're sending me home, and—"

"Hulk has been reassigned."

"Sir, can you please make an exception and have him discharged into my custody?"

The staff sergeant frowned, and a quick flicker of anger lit his eyes, but quickly disappeared. "I've heard about you two, Doodley, and I'm sorry. Hulk's a combatant, a soldier just like everyone else here. I can't just discharge him from duty. No one can."

"What if I buy him, sir? Please?"

The staff sergeant took off his hat and wiped the sweat off his brow. "No one can sell him to you; no one has that authority. A dog like that is a hundred and fifty Gs; I doubt you can rake up that kind of cash anyway. Let him go. Just... go home, get better, and start living your life."

It took all Doodley's willpower not to let his frustrated tears show. "I'll be back, sir, I swear I'll be back."

The staff sergeant drew a deep breath of air before speaking. "Sure, son, whatever you say. We'll be here."

It took two weeks before he was fitted with a prosthetic for his right leg. He signed up for a couple of trials and swallowed all sorts of junk, just to get his hands on top-notch hardware, not the typical Veterans Affairs stuff. Three more weeks of intensive physical training came after that, while he dulled the pain with a clench of his teeth and tightened fists. One more week, waiting in line to navigate the Integrated Disability Evaluation System. When he finally passed that, he went straight to reindoctrination, where he spent another two endless weeks.

He counted every day, every hour, every minute. When he finally boarded the flight to Kandahar, he could barely contain his joy. He was going to see Hulk again. Soon.

His old unit had a new sergeant, and only Adams was still there from the previous crew. Of course, the schmuck didn't know anything about Hulk, and the dog was nowhere to be found. The new sergeant was less than helpful; all he cared about was that he got a new Marine assigned to his unit, and he wasn't happy at all to get a crippled one.

"But, sir, the reason why I reenlisted was to get my dog back, Hulk," he explained, and kept insisting until the sergeant lost it and threatened him with reprimand.

He was going nowhere.

When he caught a moment, he snuck out and rushed to see the staff sergeant; at least he would remember him, and the conversation they had right before leaving Kandahar two months earlier.

He remembered just fine, but seemed rather irritated by the whole situation. "This is the US Army, Doodley, not some pet adoption center."

After yelling at him for a minute or so, the staff sergeant cooled off enough to be helpful. "He was reassigned, if I remember correctly. Yes, see here?" He shuffled some papers. "But says here he's been discharged."

Doodley's heart stopped. "Why? Was he injured?"

"No… says here he's no longer fit for duty. He's in storage on the west side of the cargo-holding area, slated for a flight stateside tomorrow morning."

He almost ran out of there without being dismissed, but stopped in the doorway, saluted, and sprinted out as soon as the staff sergeant waved him away with a scoff.

There was a corporal at the cargo area, the type who brings more embarrassment than pride to the armed forces. Doodley pleaded with him, begged, even offered to bribe him, but did little more than aggravate the man. If Doodley didn't have proper paperwork, he couldn't inspect the cargo.

He eventually left the cargo-holding area under threat of imprisonment, but didn't make it far before a young private whistled after him. He turned, surprised anyone knew him anymore. It was a stranger's face, displaying two strings of incredibly white teeth.

"You're Dood, with the dog, right?"

"Right," he replied. "Do you know where—"

"Yeah, he's in there. But, hey, be smart about it, Dood. Don't go in there asking about your dog, all emotional about it, all right? This is the Army. Just wait 'til that a-hole ends his shift, in about an hour or so, then go in there and say you're there about K9 Unit number so-and-so, you feel me?"

"Thanks," he said, and patted the young private on his shoulder. "You saved my life."

"That dog, he ain't doing that well, you know. Glad you're here."

An endless hour later, he was shown to Hulk's kennel. A shadow of what he used to be, Hulk lay in a corner, curled up, his ribs protruding through his skin. He didn't even open his eyes when Doodley approached.

He swallowed hard and tightened his fists. "What happened to this K9 unit?" he managed to ask in an impassible voice.

"How the hell should I know?" the new corporal replied. "Says here it's unfit for service, not eating, that kind of shit. If not eating would get my ass outta here, I wouldn't touch that shit for a month!"

He felt like strangling the man. Luckily, the corporal went away and sat behind his desk, immediately immersed in a phone game.

Doodley opened the kennel and gently sat next to Hulk. The dog opened his eyes and stared at him, in disbelief.

"Yeah, Hulkie, buddy, it's me. It's me," he repeated. He lifted Hulk gently and wrapped his arms around him, and felt the dog sigh, a long, pained, trembling breath of air leaving his chest with a heave.

They stayed like that for a while, and even the night-shift corporal decided to mind his own business and let them be. Then Doodley took out a combat meal package, one of those tasteless field rations he carried around with him, and shredded the wrapper with his teeth.

"What do you say we eat something, huh?"

The dog wagged his tail a little, and accepted a piece of food from Doodley's hand. Soon, he'd eaten the whole thing and licked his nose, wanting more.

Doodley showed Hulk both his empty hands. "That's all I had, buddy, but I'll get you some more. Only I got to ask you something, okay?"

Hulk sat on his tail, his ears perked up, paying attention to every word.

"You see, I sort of reenlisted to come back here for you, so if you go stateside now, we're both screwed. What do you say? Huh? Wanna give the Marine Corps another try?"

Hulk tilted his head in a gesture that Doodley remembered well. Hulk was ready to work, ready to follow him, ready to protect the unit.

"You got it… We better not get blown up again this time, you hear me?" He stood and left the kennel, locking the door behind him. "Give me a second, okay? I'll be right back," he promised, seeing the growing worry in the dog's eyes.

He went to the corporal's desk. "There's been an error. K9 Unit 36358 is not to be sent stateside. He's due for another tour of duty. I'll hold on to his discharge paperwork, but he's going back to work, effective immediately."

"Whatever you say," the corporal replied, not lifting his eyes from his phone. "Just sign the register."

Doodley walked out with Hulk on a leash, trotting toward the base. It was the wrong time and the wrong place to enjoy anything, but he relished the dusty gusts of wind from the desert, the deep purple hues of the evening sky, and the smell of dog that traveled with them. This time, he didn't contain the smile that swelled his heart.

ELMO

He kept his eyes on her while loading the dishwasher. Dishes had piled up in the sink while he'd been out of town, working his circuit of sales events and rural demos of mechanized farm equipment. Of tractors, combines, ploughs, harrows, and rotators.

How on earth did he end up selling farm equipment? He remembered the time he was excited to go out and see all those places he'd never been before. Then came the hate... He hated the machinery, the endless hours behind the wheel in the dead of winter, or crammed inside an airliner full of people. Finally, he'd grown numb, unable to feel anything anymore. He was all tapped out.

He watched her sit on the bench in the backyard, turned away from him, gesturing gently and bobbing her head on occasion. He let out a long sigh... Mother was aging faster than he liked to admit. But talking to herself was a new one. As far as he could tell, her mind was still there, intact, or almost. Sure, her memory had given a little, but her reasoning was still sharp, like in the days when she caught him lying at the first fibbing word that came out of his mouth.

Fond memories tugged at the corner of his mind, and he watched her some more, smiling gently. The backyard was serene, surrounded by trees they'd planted together, the three of them, back when they still used to be three. His late wife had chosen that bench and told him precisely where she wanted it, right under the sycamore, its backrest touching the massive tree trunk. Now his mother sat there on the wrought-iron contraption, enjoying the backyard he'd created but never had the time to use.

He focused on the dishes again, this time bringing some elbow grease to scrape a burnt saucepan. Finally satisfied, he placed it into the dishwasher just as Mother entered through the back door, a little hesitant on her feet. He frowned, concerned.

"Who were you talking to?"

"Elmo," she replied with a chuckle. "He's the only one who listens to me these days."

"Who's Elmo?"

"Ah, just a doggie. He comes and sits on that flat boulder, the one between the hydrangea bushes. I guess it's warm there. He tilts his head when I speak. He's so cute!"

He turned the water off and wiped his hands, hiding his deepening frown.

"Mother, there's no dog in our backyard. We don't have a dog."

She stomped her foot slightly and walked away angrily.

"You don't believe me. You never do. Only Elmo listens to me these days, I'm telling you."

"Okay… where is he coming from, this dog?"

"I don't know… from somewhere."

"You're not making sense, Mother, I'm sorry." He really was sorry, sorry for the lucidity that seemed to leave her mind at a hurried pace. "Our backyard is fully fenced. There's no dog."

She suddenly started crying, running her wrinkled hands through her snow-white hair and turning her face away from him.

"You never believe me anymore, never."

He swallowed a painful sigh.

"What kind of dog is Elmo?" he asked, hoping he'd pacify her.

"Don't patronize me," she snapped between tears. "You don't believe me anyway."

"Please, Mother."

She pursed her lips before continuing.

"He's small, brownish, with some black too, mostly on his back. He's a fluffy little thing, funny as hell."

He couldn't think of anything he might say to her. Imaginary dogs? Burnt pans? Three days worth of dirty dishes in the sink? How much longer could he hope to keep her home and still find her in one piece upon his return? Many elderly people were at risk of kitchen fires, of falls, or medical emergencies. With no one there to help, that could be a death sentence. She wasn't safe living on her own anymore, and he couldn't stay home with her. He took in a deep breath that burned his throat like acid.

"Mother, we need to talk."

She looked him in the eye and understood immediately what he meant.

"No... No... You promised me! Don't put me in one of those places! I won't talk to Elmo anymore, I swear!"

It took him a few days of pure hell to go through with his decision, believing with all his being that he was doing the right thing. Finally, he hit the road again, hoping that work would somehow erase the image of his brokenhearted mother from his memory, as she stared at him with mournful eyes, without saying a word, clutching the cell phone he'd bought for her.

Work didn't purge his mind and left him tossing and turning every night between the hotel bed sheets, unable to rest. On Sunday night, he caught a flight home and managed to get some shuteye in his own bed, but only after deciding to pay Mother a visit the very next day.

He was ready to go on Monday morning, fully dressed, hot cup of coffee in his hands, but he delayed leaving, engulfed in guilt. What else could he tell her to make it better? He paced the backyard, where she used to hang out, missing her deeply. He'd come home to clean dishes the night before, but he'd also come home to an empty shell, a house without a soul.

His phone rang, and he pulled it out of his pocket, frowning at the unfamiliar caller ID on the screen. A number from Kansas, where he'd just wrapped up a show.

"Hello," he said, then absentmindedly listened to a potential customer express his concerns with investing a fortune in a piece of equipment he only needed two weeks per year.

The customer wouldn't stop talking, and he kept interjecting "uh-huh" every now and then. He paced the yard for a while, phone at his ear, then sat on the bench and closed his eyes, hoping the caller would soon be gone. But no... the caller finally finished his diatribe and asked him about payment plans. He started reciting the options, terms, and qualifying factors. He opened his eyes and focused; the call could end up in a sale after all, and the commission was good, making all the travel worthwhile.

A quick movement caught his eye, and he turned toward the hydrangeas, in full blossom that early fall. He continued his sales pitch unperturbed, but his eyes searched the thick greenery. Between two of the flowering bushes, there was a flat rock, where the sun's rays landed, making their way between the sycamore's branches. On that rock, eyes locked on his and tilting his head, sat a little dog, a Yorkie by the looks of it. He wagged his tiny tail constantly and made all kinds of head movements, as he heard his voice.

He choked, losing his train of thought with the caller.

"Sir, I'm going to have to call you back," he managed, then hung up without waiting for a response. "Hello, Elmo," he said, crouching and reaching out to the dog. "You have no idea just how happy I am to meet you."

Then he tapped a couple of times on the screen of his phone, retrieving a number.

"Mother? Why don't you pack up your stuff? I'm coming to take you home."

PAY IT FORWARD

The postman read the addressee on the envelope, scribbled in large, hesitant, cursive scrawl, and then quickly checked his surroundings before pocketing the letter. He was breaking federal law right then and there, and he knew that quite well, per his postal service training. Mail theft was a federal offense, and had been ever since he could remember, yet it hadn't stopped him before. Not in the past fourteen years, since his daughter got married.

She'd met the man who later became her husband in a Home Depot store, out of all places. She wandered around, dreaming of a firepit for their backyard, and the young cowboy shopped by the cartful for all sorts of hard-to-find items, the kind that never made the shelves at the local feed store near his ranch. All it took was one long glance, or so she'd told everyone who wanted to listen, speaking about the young man with a smile in her voice and a sparkle in her eyes.

She was beautiful, his daughter, and she made a delightful bride, only a few weeks after the blushing, unexpectedly shy cowboy had asked for her hand in marriage. Soon she was gone, following her heart to an isolated horse ranch in Montana. He missed her dearly, but he was happy for her, because he knew that finding the love of one's life isn't a given.

He'd banked all his vacation time that year, and come December, he packed a few days' worth of clothing, including his down parka that rarely saw the light of day in mild-weathered Portland, and hit the road, not before changing the oil in his old Ford.

After he passed through Spokane, the road turned treacherous, and the Rockies, already covered in snow, showed the traveler no mercy. The asphalt was icy, then a snow squall blew in, an angry, relentless storm dumping inch after inch of snow and hiding the road from view.

He'd dropped speed gradually, until he barely crawled at about twenty miles per hour, but he still couldn't see where the road ended and the ditch started. He thought the road went straight, but then the wind blew clear the falling flakes, and he noticed the snow stakes marked a right, tight turn. He hit the brakes too hard. His truck skidded sideways, out of control, then stopped in the ditch, landing softly, on the blown snow accumulated there.

He drew a deep breath, and let it out with a slew of cuss words, then hopped out of his truck, landing in 3 feet of the puffy white stuff. He tried his cell phone, but there wasn't any signal out there between the mountains. Resigned to having to wait until morning, half buried in snow, he climbed back into the truck and slammed the door shut.

He'd dozed off when a man banged on his window. With few words and fewer gestures, the stranger hooked the truck to his own and pulled him out of the ditch. Thankful, the postman offered him cash, but the country man declined with a quick headshake.

"Pay it forward," he'd said, taking two fingers to the rim of his hat, then disappeared into the whiteout, toward Spokane.

He drove the rest of the way to his daughter's ranch without incident, and by the time he got there, he'd made a commitment. Every time someone showed him kindness, he'd put five dollars into a jar. Then he would answer someone's prayer with that money in December. What better way to do that, than opening the poorly addressed, insufficiently stamped letters to Santa?

It's true that he did have to steal them to be able to answer them. Minor detail, major federal offense. But no one missed those letters anyway, and, year after year, he got away with it.

He'd started small at first, and he still remembered that his first year pay-it-forward fund held thirty dollars. It made him sad to think he'd encountered kindness only six times during the entire year. But then, each year, the jar filled faster, and so did his heart, waiting for Christmas.

It was December again, and once he got home, he opened the letter he'd pocketed on his route and read it carefully, struggling with the poor spelling of the child who'd written it by himself.

"Dear Santa," the letter read, "Please get me a doctor for my mommy. A bad man took her purse and beat her. She can't go to the doctor because there is no money. Her hand hurts."

He sighed, then typed a reply in the form of an advertising letter, advising the mother of the existence of a victim compensation program in their county and how to enroll and get free medical assistance. Sometimes, the gift of his knowledge was better than the small amount of money he had to offer.

He opened another letter, read it twice, the second time thinking hard. The sender, a little girl named Sandy, asked for a computer to help her daddy get a job. She swore she'd been a good girl the whole year, and her daddy had been good too.

With a sad smile, the postman examined the envelope. Sandy had scribbled the return address on it, but hadn't affixed any stamps, and just addressed it simply, "To: Santa Claus, North Pole." The letter would have never made it anywhere, not even to the postal service "Letters to Santa Program," but he knew where the family lived. He knew the little girl, and he'd noticed the man's car hadn't left the driveway in a while.

He emptied the jar and counted the money. Almost three hundred dollars in there; it had been a kind year. It was enough to get a small laptop and a few months' worth of Internet service. But he didn't stop there; he called a couple of friends and asked them if they were willing to put in some pro-bono work. Then he wrote a detailed letter to go with the computer, offering assistance with résumé building and career counseling, courtesy of his friends.

The postman was tired the next day, as he made his rounds and delivered high volumes of holiday season mail. He'd been up half the night, getting everything ready to make Sandy's wish come true. A little distracted, he drove from mailbox cluster to mailbox cluster, ignoring the cold wind, thinking of the steaming coffee he was going to get on his lunch break. He didn't notice the little boy who sat on the curb waiting for him. He just shoved envelopes in the mailboxes and was almost ready to lock the mailbox cluster, when the little boy's voice got his attention.

"Hello, Mr. Postman," he said, shyly.

He turned and smiled at the boy. "Hello, young man."

"May I please ask you something?"

The boy, not a day older than eight, shifted his weight from one foot to the other, keeping his hands buried in the pockets of his wet coat.

He dropped the parcel he was holding back into the postal truck, and nodded vigorously. "Shoot."

"Can you please not bring these letters anymore? They make my mommy cry."

The boy held out an empty, crumpled envelope, bearing the stamp, "Final Notice," in bright, red letters.

He swallowed hard, then put his hand on the boy's shoulder. "How about your daddy?"

"He's gone," the boy whispered, lowering his head. "It's just mommy and me now."

He frowned, thinking hard. Life's tragedies hit in so many flavors, it was hard to guess which one had struck that little boy's family. "Where does your mother go to work?"

"She stays home with me now," he said, avoiding his glance. "They didn't need her anymore at the factory."

He stood there in the biting cold, speechless, thinking hard. Then he made his decision. "Okay, son, let me see what I can do," he said, and patted the boy on his shoulder.

He spent his lunch hour digging up the woman's phone number and interviewing her, under false pretenses, to find out the reason for her unemployment. He broke a lot of laws that day.

It was the same story, only with a different mailing address. A laid-off single parent, condemned to a slow and painful descent into despondence and desperation, by a decision someone had made without knowing, without caring. Then the struggle to survive, in a world that had rapidly changed and demanded everything digital, from online profiles to email résumés and Web application forms, just to gain access to blue-collar jobs.

The postman ended the call and rubbed his forehead for a long minute, ashamed he didn't have two jars of three hundred dollars each. Humiliated he had to choose between the two families. He stared at the stained cafeteria table for a long time, but when he lifted his eyes and looked outside the window, it was snowing hard. It was coming down heavily, like that night, many years ago, when he'd crossed the Rockies to see his daughter.

He smiled at the falling snow, so rare an occurrence in Portland, and then looked at the time. He still had twenty minutes before having to resume his route. Plenty of time to post numerous ads for snow removal, for twenty dollars per driveway, on every site he could think of. He only needed to do fifteen of those to get the money he needed.

He called a few friends who didn't mind the fresh-air exercise, and by the end of the evening, he had the money. He was tired, and his bones ached, but he slept like a baby, knowing the next morning that he'd only have to deliver two packages, before hitting the road to go visit his daughter.

Because the next morning, the postal service was going to be closed. For Christmas Day.

HOME

Anne drove over the speed limit, keeping it low enough to avoid getting caught, but pushing it as fast as she could. At least she hoped she wouldn't end up seeing the blue lights in her rearview mirror, further delaying her from reaching home. Squinting in the sunlight, she searched the stretch of Interstate ahead of her, almost completely devoid of traffic, and pushed the pedal a bit more. The speedometer added a few more miles per hour, going above eighty-five in a seventy-five zone. There better not be any cops hidden somewhere in those bushes, waiting cowardly like spiders for someone like her, doing nothing wrong other than rushing to get home.

She didn't know what had happened, and flurries of anxiety swarmed in her gut, while she worried mile after mile. Her grandmother, the only family she had left, lived alone on the Redstone, Colorado, horse farm that had been her home her entire life. She was headstrong yet frail, adamantly refusing any live-in help. Anne called her every day, either during her lunch break at the hospital, or from her drive home to the small Denver apartment she shared with Derek. She'd just called Gran the night before, and she gave her the usual small talk: nothing was wrong, everything was fine, fields were green this time of year, horses were happy, all was good. Just peachy.

Only she'd lied.

Or so it seemed, until Anne had run into someone from Redstone, an old, arthritic man who lived over the ridge from their farm. What was his name? She believed it was Joe, Joe Buchanan, maybe? Or was it Jim? Maybe it was Jim.

Whatever-his-name-was chastised her openly in the middle of a busy hospital hallway, for abandoning her home, her last remaining family, for not caring that the farm was being foreclosed, that her own grandmother was dying. Anne didn't ask any questions. Blood turned to ice in her veins, she left an incoherent message to her boss then rushed out the door and burned rubber on her way out of the parking lot. That had happened four hours ago.

As she drove, she'd been dying to call Gran and question her on the state of her health, on the fate of the family farm, on the reasons behind her lies. Instead, she refrained from speed-dialing her number, and opted to call the bank instead.

Just getting to speak to a person who was able and willing to answer some basic questions about the farm's mortgage took Anne almost fifty miles of highway, driven over the speed limit while listening to horrible, looping, hold music sprinkled with shameless self-serving advertising, including her all-time favorites, the messages intended to get callers to hang up and find service online or through methods that didn't require bank employees to take their calls.

Finally, after she'd just passed Copper Mountain, she was connected with a bored, middle-aged man, by the sound of his voice, and she made a split-second decision and started to identify herself with her grandmother's name and details, unwilling to be told that mortgage information was confidential and couldn't be disclosed to anyone other than the homeowner.

She recited from memory her grandmother's full name, the farm's address, her social security number, everything the man wanted to verify. Finally, he had her on hold while he reviewed her records, and she waited, tension building in her shoulders, while she watched the fluctuating bars of cell phone signal shift with every turn of the road. Thankfully, the call didn't disconnect, and eight endless minutes later, the man eventually spoke.

"I'm actually surprised you're not aware of your situation Miss, um, Miller. We've sent you correspondence that wasn't returned. I see here, um, at least seven letters sent in the past four months."

"I know that," Anne managed to say, almost deafened by the sound of her own thumping heart. "I'm old, you see," she added, letting her voice tremble without trying to control it anymore. "Can you please tell me what the situation is, right now? How much do I owe?"

A moment of silence filled the airwaves, and the occasional keyboard tap was the only sound she heard.

"With penalties, late fees, and everything, your total loan balance is $41,568.93. Unless you bring your account to current status, we'll start foreclosure proceedings in six days."

"You're taking the farm?" Anne asked in disbelief. "All of it? For forty grand?"

The property sprawled over thirty-five acres of green pastures tucked between rocky hills and reaching all the way to the steep mountain versants. The main building was old, but had kept its charm, even after Anne's father had completely remodeled it. He'd stripped it to the core, bringing the benefits of modernity in the form of new wiring, new plumbing, tiles throughout the kitchen and bathrooms, new windows, and an additional parking space in the garage. All that, without taking away any of its charm, any of its personality. Twenty years had passed since then.

"Um, yeah, all of it," the banking representative replied, dispersing Anne's memories and bringing her back to reality.

She grunted and repressed a sigh. "There must be something we can do, right? Please."

"Yeah, you can pay," the man replied in a voice that couldn't have sounded more indifferent.

"Six days, you said?" she confirmed. "Until next Wednesday?"

"Correct."

"All right, thank you," she replied, then cut the call from her steering wheel button, wishing there could have been something she could throw and smash, something that would shatter into millions of pieces to appease her anguish.

Forty thousand dollars? How was she going to get all that money? She'd barely finished her residency, and had taken an ER anesthesiologist job at the University of Colorado Hospital, barely making enough to cover her crippling student loan payments and to save for a down payment on their home. Their home... hers and Derek's.

She'd met him during her second year of residency, and their romance had been intense, all-consuming, despite being squeezed between long hospital hours and conflicting shifts. When they'd managed to schedule the first getaway together for a week in Cabo, they both slept through the first half of the week, enjoying the closeness yet yielding to the demands of their exhausted bodies.

When Derek proposed a few months later, she'd been the happiest girl on campus, smiling widely for days in a row, despite working long shifts in the emergency room. They were made for each other, she and Derek. They understood each other and had many things in common, the healthy foundation of an enduring friendship to base their marriage on.

A couple of months were left until the date they chose together, and very little to plan for. Both practical and both broke, they'd decided to have a simple ceremony for close friends and family in Denver, then take a few days to enjoy each other on the Redstone farm. When she'd suggested a pastoral honeymoon, she'd never imagined the farm could no longer be theirs.

With cold, trembling fingers she pressed the call button on her steering wheel and said, "Call Derek's cell." The call went straight to voicemail; probably he was still in surgery.

"Hi, it's me," she whispered after the machine beeped. "I'm on my way home," she said hesitantly, then stopped. Derek thought of their Denver apartment as being their home. "To Redstone, that home," she chuckled sadly. "Something's wrong, I don't know what exactly, but I'll call you later and we'll talk." She stopped for a second, almost ready to blurt out all her fears, her unspoken turmoil. Instead, she decided to wait until she could speak with him, the actual, living, breathing man she loved, not a stupid machine. "Bye for now."

She tightened the grip on the steering wheel and scrutinized the highway ahead of her, then gave the cruise control setting a couple of more miles. She checked the time and mumbled a curse. Another hour and a half to go, of not knowing. Her mind blanked, and memories started coming back, things she didn't even think she still remembered.

Her father teaching her how to ride a horse. The day she climbed on the back of a horse by herself, without assistance. The stormy night when the sheriff's knock on the door informed the little girl her father wasn't coming back. Visiting his grave with Gran, while she held Gran's hand tightly, afraid to let go, and wondering why her mother's stone looked so much darker than her father's. Her high school prom, holding the arm of a freckled boy by the name of Caleb; she remembered not liking him too much, but he'd been the only one who'd asked her. Boys were a little afraid of her back then. Then medical school in Denver, and, of course, Derek.

She almost missed the exit but compensated at the last second and left I-70 among a couple of honking horns and screeching tires. She headed south toward Redstone, cutting through Glenwood Springs without slowing down too much. Through some miracle, she managed to make it out of town without getting pulled over, and soon she was hitting the state highway along the Roaring Fork River east bank, enjoying the view and not minding the speedometer much.

That's when she heard it, the distinctive blare of a police siren. She cursed under her breath and pulled over, then waited for a few long minutes for the cop to make his way to her car.

The officer wore the uniform of Pitkin County Sheriff's Office. Good, at least her speeding ticket money would support the local economy. She rolled down her window and attempted to smile, but she was too worried to manage much of a smile.

"Officer," she said, feeling angst choking her.

"Driver's license and registration, please," he said coldly.

He checked her ID quickly, then looked at her. "Do you know why I stopped you?"

"I believe I do, Officer, and I apologize. I'm a doctor, and I was notified there's a problem with my grandmother, who lives alone on the Cold Creek Horse Farm. You might know it."

The officer glared at her. "So, you're Ellen Miller's granddaughter?"

She nodded, frowning slightly, confused by his reaction and his knowledge of her grandmother's name.

"Well, it's about time someone hurried that way," he replied, handing her back the license and registration. "Keep it below fifty-five."

He nodded once, then turned and disappeared before she could regain her voice to thank him. She started her engine and rolled away, refraining from stepping on it in the first few minutes, but moving the needle to sixty-five miles per hour as soon as she was out of the cop's direct line of sight.

The sheriff's office knew about Gran? What the hell was going on back home?

Her frown deepened and she reached for the car's display to make the call she'd been postponing. The hell with it; she needed to know. But Derek's name popped up on the screen just as the familiar ringtone resounded in the car.

"Hey, Derek," she said, sounding weird and out of breath. "You heard my message?"

"I did," he replied. She could hear the tension in his voice. "What's going on?"

"I don't really know yet. The farm is being foreclosed, and it seems like Gran isn't doing all that well." As she spoke the words, things became real, as real as they get when shared with a loved one. Tears streamed down her cheeks, streaking burning marks in her casual, light makeup.

"We just spoke with her..." Derek said, sounding both surprised and worried.

"I know," she whispered. "She lied. I shouldn't have believed her. I should've come here more often, to check on her, on everything."

"When? You've been working sixty-hour weeks since last Thanksgiving."

She didn't say anything, just sniffled quietly as Derek made her excuses, words she didn't want to hear.

"Call me and let me know what's going on," he added quietly. "Let me know what you need."

She hung up after thanking him, unable to tell him how badly she needed him, how scared she was. How desperately she hoped Gran was all right, there for her like she'd always been, her only family.

She recognized a few buildings in the early dusk and slowed a bit, entering Redstone and driving through without stopping, eager to get home. Then she took a right turn after leaving Redstone, heading toward the farm, on the last stretch of road.

As she approached the familiar grounds, she recognized everything. The way the road curved up the hill; the white ranch rail fences that any horse could jump over, yet none of them did; the majestic main building in white stucco, with black accents; and the black garage doors and the large stables adjacent to the main building.

Then she slowed and her breath caught. One by one, the familiar things she recognized, she didn't recognize anymore. The stables were in shambles, the roof collapsed on one side. The house was dark, enshrouded in stillness, despite the early evening hour. A single horse stood behind the fence, a black stallion with a white star on his forehead.

"Flicker," Anne whispered, bringing her car to a stop next to the fence. She jumped out and trotted toward the horse. He walked toward her with a snort, recognizing her, and Anne noticed his head bobbed with every step, a sign of lameness she couldn't pinpoint. He must be old by now; he was the horse she'd learned to ride as a young child.

She touched Flicker's nose and patted his neck, then rushed toward the house. Right there, on the patio, in front of the main door, there was a potted rose in bloom, and next to it, a gardening trowel. Her grandmother, unaware of her presence, appeared from inside the house and bent forward with difficulty to pick up the potted rose.

"Put down that damn rose right now," Anne shouted angrily, "or I'll smash the thing into a million pieces!"

Startled, the old woman looked up, and her face lit up with a million wrinkles when she smiled. "Anne! My baby!"

Anne rushed to hug her tightly, letting her tears run freely. "Why did you lie to me? Why didn't you tell me about the farm?"

"Let me look at you," Gran said, pulling herself away and measuring Anne from head to toe. "Look how beautiful you are!"

"Yeah, okay. Why did you lie to me? I called you every day, and you... Where are all the horses?"

Gran's smile died and she turned her head away. "You have your life to live, my dear. In the city, with your young man, doing what you always wanted to do. What you're good at doing, being a doctor. You have no time for me, and that's the way it should be. New replaces old, it's the circle of life."

Probably feeling a little weak from all the excitement, Gran sat in an Adirondack chair, holding on to the arms with both hands. Anne crouched next to her and took her hand.

"Talk to me. What happened?"

"Last winter… they stole the horses."

"Who?"

"Some men just came one night and took all of them. Even Flicker, but he came back after a few days." Gran wiped a tear from the corner of her eye with the back of her hand.

"Did they catch them?"

"They did, but the horses were gone. The sheriff drove here himself to tell me."

"I was here in March, Gran. That happened after March?"

Gran threw her a quick, guilty gaze. "No… in January."

"And you didn't bother to tell me?" She stood and paced the porch with angry, heavy steps.

"You arrived late at night, slept the whole time, then left the next day, also after dark. You were so tired. I didn't have the heart."

"Damn…" she muttered, then continued pacing the porch, her heavy steps against the wood resounding strangely into the evening silence.

No horses meant no income for the farm. No wonder Gran had fallen behind on the mortgage.

"Everybody knows you're in trouble, except for me, Gran. How do you think that makes me feel? I want to be here for you, to help you."

"Who is everyone?"

"That guy, Jim Buchanan?" Anne said, pointing vaguely in the direction of the Buchanan farm.

"Ah, you mean Joe. He helped me clean things up, after the horses were gone."

"And what about the sheriff's deputy?" Anne asked, but immediately knew the answer. Her grandmother had been robbed; of course, the cops knew about it.

"Them too," Gran said, nodding slightly.

"And what the hell is with this thing here?" Anne said, stomping her foot hard right next to the potted rose.

"You know what this is, sweetie," Gran said gently. "It's time."

"The hell it is!" she snapped.

"Our family has had this farm since 1852, you know. Since then, all women in the family plant this one rose when the time has come for them to—"

"Don't want to hear it. I know the damn legend, and I know how far back our history goes. I only wish the mortgage would've been paid off by now."

"You know about that too, don't you?" Gran whispered, clutching her arthritic hands together in her lap. "Your father took that mortgage when he rebuilt the house."

She nodded a few times. "Don't care about the damn tradition. It stopped with my mother. Period. She didn't plant her rose."

"No. Your father planted it for her. The crimson one, the last in line." Gran closed her eyes and leaned back, silent for a while. "What's your middle name, Anne?"

"It's Rose, you know that," she replied, confused.

"And you probably know mine," Gran added.

"I thought I was named after you and my paternal grandmother. But I always wondered why they gave me her first name, Anne, and your middle name, Rose. Not Ellen, your first name, but Rose. I was glad though, because it was also my mother's—"

She stopped abruptly, under her grandmother's blue gaze. "I didn't realize it until now. Were we all named Rose? Why?"

Gran smiled and her lips trembled a little when she spoke.

"You see that rose garden, at the side of the house? Stefan Miller started that garden with one white bloom, in 1863. He arrived here with his beloved wife, Sara Rose, just two German immigrants chasing the gold dream, trying their luck on Pikes Peak. They found a few nuggets, enough to start this farm."

Anne remembered hearing bits and pieces of the story before, but she'd never really paid attention. Now she was all ears, while a million questions popped into her mind.

"Why did they stop mining? If they found gold?"

"It was hard rock mining, not easy at the time. The shallow gold deposits vanished quickly, and there were many other gold miners, some of them violent brutes with nothing to lose. Then Sara Rose fell ill one winter; her lungs."

Anne didn't dare interrupt with her questions; there would be time for those later.

"She died that winter, in her husband's arms, while their two sons were away fighting the Apaches in the Southwest." Gran stood slowly, holding on to the chair for balance, then reaching out to grab Anne's extended arm. Together, they walked to the far end of the porch, toward the rose garden. "I guess modern medicine would call what happened to Stefan that day a heart attack or something; you probably know better. Story goes that he barely had the strength to bury his wife here, next to the house, then he died right there, next to the rose he'd planted on her grave."

Anne turned and looked her grandmother in the eye.

"You mean to tell me someone's buried in our yard? Sara Rose Miller lays there?"

"Both of them are, my dear."

Anne's hand flew to her mouth, as to withhold a gasp. "There's no headstone, nothing to mark their grave."

"Look more carefully," Gran said with a quiet smile.

Anne leaned over the porch railing, staring behind the big rose bush at the end of the patch, where a boulder stood, darkened by time.

"That was enough, back in the old days, you know. And so, a tradition was born. All Miller women bear the middle name Rose, in Sara Rose's memory, and in the hope that every one of us will be loved the way she was."

Anne smiled. It was a charming story, despite learning that the rose garden was also a grave. She walked over to the potted rose and propped her hands on her hips. "And what's up with this?"

"It's my time now."

"Pfft," Anne scoffed, "no, it's not. Are you sick? Why do you keep saying it's your time?"

"They're taking the farm. I can't lose all this," Gran said, then turned away to hide the tears that trembled in her voice.

Anne let a long breath escape her lungs.

"Let's get us some dinner, Gran. The rose can wait in its pot until morning, then we'll find a place for it, but I promise you it won't be in that rose garden. Not yet."

They ate a simple dinner quietly, with few words spoken between them.

Later, she cried, locked in her old bedroom, face buried in the pillow, ignoring Derek's voicemails and text messages until one caught her attention. It read, "I'm freaking out, so I'm coming over." She called him right away, although it was almost three in the morning.

"What's going on?" he said without any introduction.

"Oh, Derek," she whispered on a loaded, pained breath. "I'm losing everything I ever had, except you. But to hold on to what I still can, I'm losing you."

"What do you mean?" he asked, and she could hear the frown in his voice.

"This is my home, baby, please understand. I won't be coming back. I can't... not for a while."

"I thought your home was here, with me, this dreary apartment we almost never get to see."

"I thought so too," she whispered. "But I just can't let go, can't let them take this away from us."

"What do you want to do?"

"I don't know, not yet. I can hold on to it for a while. I can pay off part of what's owed with what I've been saving for our house, but then—"

"Then what? There's no job for you there, no future, no money. I'm not there either."

"I can't ask you to come with me. You're a surgeon, there's nothing here for you."

"There's nothing there for you either, Anne."

"I could go into general practice. There are almost two hundred people who live in the area. I'm sure they'd like to have a doctor nearby."

"Almost two hundred, huh? And what, they'll pay you in chickens?"

She whimpered, feeling the hurt in his words.

"I need to do this for a while, until I know Gran will be okay. Until I know that she's safe. Then I'll work weekdays in Denver, and spend the weekends in Redstone, taking whatever patients I can scare up."

He didn't speak for a while, and neither did she, happy to just breathe in unison with him. Happy to know he was there.

"How about us, Anne?" he asked quietly. "What happened with, 'home is where you'll be'"?

"Please... Wait for me if you can. I just need a little time, to sort things out here," she added, feeling choked, unable to breathe.

"I thought we were getting married in a couple of months," Derek replied. "Are you breaking up with me?"

"No, I promise you I'm not. I just can't leave her... can't leave my home. I have to be away from you right now, but I love you more than ever. Please know that."

He didn't say anything, only waited for her to say something else, but she couldn't find words. She just whispered, "Good night," then hung up the phone and buried her face back into the tear-soaked pillow.

Anne woke with a start the next morning to the sound of nails being driven into wood. The sun was up, and she jumped out of bed, reciting the mental to-do list she'd prepared. Negotiate with the bank the minimum amount that would bring their loan current. Evaluate the damage to the property and identify any emergencies. Give Gran a physical, just in case her rose-planting urges were more physiologically motivated. Make sure she didn't plant the damn rose in the "graveyard garden," as she'd just dubbed it the night before. Give Flicker a physical too, with a bit of help from a friend, because the town's only vet had recently passed away. Figure out her future. Easy list; she should be done by noon.

She stepped out on the porch looking for Gran and found her by the stairs, holding a cup of hot tea in her trembling hands and looking up at the man making all the noise. She stepped in front of the house to see what was going on and couldn't distinguish who the man was, his silhouette barely visible against the bright morning sun. But her eyes fell on the sign he'd just hung, right above the door. It was nothing but a rectangular piece of plywood, probably painted in a hurry by someone who'd never painted a sign before.

It read, "Walk-In Clinic. Drs. Miller and Thomas. New Patients Welcome." She gave a sharp, guttural sound. "Derek!" she called, rushing toward the foot of the ladder.

He climbed down and lifted her in his arms. "Like?"

She kissed him before replying, taking her time, savoring her joy.

"You can't be serious, baby," she said.

"Home is where you'll be, right? Just the weekends for now. I'll gladly take Anthem Blue Cross, Medicare, and chickens too."

She snuck her arm around his waist. "Yes, but will you double as a vet?"

"Why?"

"I've got a horse that needs your attention."

"Sure, why not? There's a first time for everything, I guess."

"Where's Gran?" she asked, then noticed the potted rose was missing from the porch. The trowel was gone too.

"Stubborn old woman and her damn rose," she muttered, then rushed to the side of the porch, looking for her in the graveyard garden. But she wasn't there.

She turned to ask Derek if he'd seen her, but saw Gran digging a hole in the ground to plant the rose, all the way over by the road, near the gate. She smiled, watching her from a distance, and her smile deepened when Derek interlaced his fingers with hers.

"What's with your grandmother and that rose?"

She laughed. "Welcome home."

HER DOG

When Sherman Hansen heard the doorbell, he rushed downstairs faster than the dog, leaping three steps at a time. Through the narrow windows that flanked the massive oak door he could see the flashing lights of the police car, sending splashes of blue and red against the white sheers.

They found her, a fleeting thought brought hope to his weary mind. *Maybe they brought her home.*

He opened the door and froze. Only those two annoying cops were there, those two idiots who just couldn't get it in their thick skulls that Dolly would never walk away from him.

"Going somewhere, Mr. Hansen?" the female cop asked him, her eyes fixed on the dog leash he clutched in his hand.

He scoffed angrily. "That's what you're here for? To ask me if I'm going somewhere?"

"No, sir," the other cop intervened. "We wanted to know if you've heard anything, or if your wife called—"

Sherman shook his head in disbelief. "You just don't get it, do you? She wasn't going to go anywhere. She told me to take her truck when I went to Rapid City, and she only does that when she's planning to stay home. I'm telling you, someone took her, and you're wasting time here, instead of looking for her."

"Are you sure?" the woman asked, her head on a swivel, studying the surroundings. His house stood on four acres of land, some of it wooded and pristine.

"Officer, um, I'm sorry, I forgot your name—"

"Detective Benton, and this is Detective Flynn," she clarified.

"So, yes, Detective Benton, I'm sure. We've been married for thirty years. Dolly would never leave the house without her truck and without Spot, her dog. End of story. Now, if you're not going to start looking for her, please leave. I'm busy."

The dog, hearing his name, wagged his stump tail a little, keeping his cautious eyes trained on the two strangers at the door. He was a four-year-old Springer Spaniel, white with brown spots, an incredible hunting dog. Dolly loved hunting ducks and pheasants with him. She loved doing everything with him.

"We can't declare an adult a missing person before twenty-four hours have passed, sir," Flynn said, hints of regret in his voice.

"But I see you've got time to kill," Hansen insisted. "I bet there's a police dog locked in some kennel in Rapid City who could use the exercise, if only someone would give a crap!"

"I'm sorry, sir, we can't, not right now. If she's not back by tomorrow morning, we'll—"

"I can't afford to wait," Hansen replied, struggling against the urge to send a slew of cuss words at the two. "Spot, come here, buddy," he called and crouched, patting the dog quickly on his head and slipping the collar and leash on him. Then he grabbed his shotgun from behind the door, a box of buckshot shells, and one of Dolly's T-shirts that he'd brought down from their bedroom.

"Where are you going, Mr. Hansen?" Benton asked.

"Hunting, can't you tell?" he threw the words at her over his shoulder in almost a growl.

"You're going to look for your wife, aren't you?" Flynn asked. "Sir, I must advise—"

He turned as if he'd been hit by something. "Don't you two dare advise me of anything, you hear me? You won't look for her, that's lame, and I'll have to live with it. But I won't sit on my hands and wait for you two to find her body in a ravine somewhere."

"If your wife was taken by someone, you would be risking your life and probably hers too," Flynn insisted. "Why don't you wait here, by the phone, and we'll talk to our sergeant to see if we can make an exception in this case."

He shook his head again and ran his hand over his mouth, trying to keep his thoughts locked inside his head.

"Yeah, you go ahead and do that, Detectives. I'm going hunting."

He crouched next to Spot and had him sniff Dolly's T-shirt. The dog whimpered quietly.

"Now, go find Mom." The dog ran outside and he followed, closing the door on the way out.

Spot seemed a little confused, and then he started sniffing the thick layer of leaves that covered the yard near the tree line. He kept pulling on the leash, like hunting dogs will do. He seemed to know where he was going, and Sherman hoped that sensitive nose of his wasn't chasing some animal or bird instead of Dolly.

He knew whoever took her hadn't come in a car; when he'd returned from Rapid City that morning and found she was gone, he inspected the driveway carefully. It wasn't surfaced; they couldn't afford that. It was covered in small pebbles and dust, the fine kind that turned to mud at the first few drops of rain, the kind that keeps tire prints really well if the wind isn't gusting. And it wasn't, not that day.

He'd looked at the driveway yard by yard, and only saw familiar tire tracks. No dusty footprints led to the front door, and he'd found that door left unlocked, which Dolly would never do. If someone had come to their front door, he must've come from the woods, stepping only on grass and keeping the fine dust off his shoes.

Why would Dolly open the door to a stranger? He tried to think of a reason, but then the obvious answer came to his mind: she probably wouldn't. She'd open the door to someone she knew, someone she recognized, like a neighbor or maybe a friend.

Right after he'd discovered she was gone, he'd called two friends who lived nearby and neither had seen her. They offered to help, and he was considering it, thinking he could cover more terrain with some assistance before sundown. But first, he'd called the cops and wasted a good half hour waiting for them to show up. Then another hour went by while giving statements and swearing he didn't kill her himself, then they finally went away, giving him time to think and get ready to search for her. Now they came by again, only to waste more of his time. Unbelievable.

He rushed through the woods, pulled by Spot who didn't hesitate, just sniffed the ground every now and then and kept on going, heading farther away from the house and into familiar hunting grounds. They lived on the outskirts of Summerset, South Dakota, their house the last one on the street, tucked against the Black Hills National Forest. They both enjoyed the peace and quiet and, until that day, he'd never regretted not having nosy neighbors constantly in his business.

Spot slowed a little and sniffed the air, as if unsure where to go from there. Dolly didn't just vanish in the middle of the woods; there wasn't any body of water nearby, not for another half-mile, but the brush had grown denser and the many smells probably confused Spot. Sherman took Dolly's T-shirt out and let the dog sniff it again, holding it against his nose. Spot buried his nose in it, inhaling the familiar scent, and then started wagging his tail, excited.

"Yes, buddy, find Mom! She's got all the good doggie food. Where's Mom?"

The dog bolted, tugging hard against the leash, and Sherman, a bit out of breath, rushed behind Spot. Seeing the spaniel so determined filled his heart with hope that he would find her soon. He couldn't think what had happened, or what he'd do once he found her. He only wanted to find her, alive, unharmed. Then he'd have plenty of time to figure things out, like who took her and why.

Twenty or so minutes later, both he and Spot were out of breath, panting hard. They came to a clearing he knew well, a place where they often set camp when deer hunting. The dog stopped and sniffed the air, and Sherman leaned forward, propping his hands against his knees, fighting to catch his breath. He managed to stop panting for a few moments and inhaled some air through his nose, catching the distant smell of barbecue, of meat roasting on coals.

He pressed Dolly's T-shirt to Spot's nose again. "Come on, little buddy, where's Mom?"

The dog zigzagged in place, confused, whimpering. Sherman offered the T-shirt again and again, encouraging the dog, but nothing. Spot didn't want to move away from that place, going in circles, his tail lowered and his enthusiasm all gone.

Sherman knew what that meant; the scent trail ended there, at the edge of that forest clearing, in the middle of the woods. He had nothing, nowhere to go. He looked around, trying to think. What could've happened to make her trail disappear? He kneeled on the grass and started examining that patch of ground, foot by foot, until he found what he was looking for.

Two sets of footprints that came from the woods, barely visible in the grass. Then only one set continued from that point forward, the larger of the two, after they'd stepped in place for a while, going in circles, just like Spot had done. Whoever had taken Dolly had chosen to carry her from that point forward, and her scent had since vanished, scattered by the gentle breeze.

He called Spot and showed the man's footprint with his

finger. "Sniff this, buddy, sniff it good. Yeah... good boy."

A little unsure at first, Spot started leading them across the clearing. As they forged ahead, the smell of barbecue became stronger, and soon he could distinguish a thin cloud of smoke in the distance, above the trees. *Must be some hunting cabin*, he thought, slowing down and tugging at the leash.

"Easy, boy," he whispered, and Spot slowed, putting slack in the leash and searching his eyes. Then he whimpered a little louder, but soon that whimper turned to a growl. Sherman clasped the leash tighter and looked for the source of his dog's anxiety.

"Howdy," a man said, almost startling him. It was a hulk of a man, about six foot four and weighing over two fifty, all muscle and prison tats. He wore a long, unkempt beard, and his hair hadn't been trimmed in a long time, probably since his release. He wore a thick belt on top of some dirty, mismatched military garb, showing off a huge hunting knife, a forty-five tucked inside that belt, and a small axe in his left hand.

"Hey," Sherman replied, still out of breath, evaluating his chances against that man. The stranger was at least twenty years younger and didn't seem the type who'd let his conscience bother him in any way. He didn't have much of a fighting chance; he needed to go a different way. "How's it going?"

"It's going," the man replied, studying Sherman with vile eyes. "Shoot anything yet?"

"Not yet," he replied, "we're just getting started."

"What you huntin' for?"

"Pheasant. Seen any?"

"Some, but ain't season yet."

Sherman smiled, feigning a little guilt. "Well, that's why I'm here, 'cause it ain't season yet. I'm guessing this far into the woods no one will hear the shots."

The stranger shrugged and frowned. "I'm here."

"And you mind?" Sherman asked, tugging gently at the leash to stop Spot from whimpering.

"Nah... knock yourself out," the man replied after a moment of hesitation, then turned around and left the way he came, into the woods due southwest.

He crouched and grabbed Spot by the collar, bringing the dog's head gently next to his. "Got to be smart, little buddy. We can't take this guy, just the two of us. Got to be real smart."

Still crouching, he took in the lay of the land. The thin cloud of smoke coming from the man's cabin could've been more than half a mile southwest. If he headed west and then south, maybe he could come on the cabin from behind and surprise him.

Then what?

Was he ready to shoot a man, without knowing whether he took his wife or not? Even if he'd known for sure, would he be able to load game shells into his shotgun and cross the line he'd never crossed before and end a man's life?

If that man had taken Dolly, hell, yeah.

He scratched Spot behind the ears for a few moments, whispering, "We have to be really quiet, buddy. You hear me? Really, really quiet." Then he stood and started west, the shotgun on his arm loaded with four buckshot shells.

They walked quickly through the thick woods, although he stopped every now and then to listen to the noises of the forest, to sniff the smoke coming from the cabin. After about twenty-five minutes, he turned left, heading south, but walked slowly and carefully not to make any noises or step on branches that could crack loudly and give him away. He expected to see the cabin at any moment.

He reached another small clearing and stopped at its edge. He could see the cabin's back wall, a hundred or so yards away. Unwilling to step into the clearing, he followed the tree line until he was about thirty feet from the cabin's back wall. He heard a radio playing country music close by, and the smells of meat juices on coals were strong now.

Spot started whimpering, tugging hard against the leash. "Quiet, Spot, quiet," Sherman whispered, and the dog obeyed, but started scratching the ground with his front paws, digging a hole in the soft soil, near what seemed like a piece of PVC pipe coming out of the ground. "Shhh... stop that," he said, tugging at the leash, but the dog wouldn't budge.

He thought for a moment what to do with Spot. He couldn't attempt to take that man while holding the leash. If he tied him to a tree trunk, Spot would soon become anxious and raise hell, baying and barking; he wasn't used to being restricted. Dolly let him run free and he always behaved. Maybe that was the way, let him run free. The dog would go straight to the man, and he'd have the element of surprise.

He detached the dog's leash from the collar and gently patted Spot on his back. The dog looked at him briefly and bolted back to the piece of PVC coming from the ground, digging desperately around it. Must've been the man's cellar, where he kept smoked venison and such. Or...

His breath caught and a wave of panic rushed through his body. What if Dolly were there, locked underground, in the man's cellar? He went next to Spot and stopped him from digging. "Easy, easy," he repeated, until the dog stopped and looked in his eyes. "Where's Mom?" Spot resumed digging furiously.

"Son of a bitch," he whispered, clutching his weapon. He snuck along the side of the cabin, one careful footstep after another, until he reached the front. He peeked from behind the wall and saw a rusted folding chair set in front of a firepit surrounded by boulders, on top of which some pieces of meat sizzled, set directly on red, hot coals. But the man was nowhere in sight.

"Hunting pheasant, huh?" he heard the man say, feeling

the cold barrel of a gun pressing hard against the back of his head. "Wanna try again; see if you fool me twice?" The man spat, then laughed, the coarse laughter of a habitual drinker. Liquor carried on the man's breath, the sour, moonshine kind. "Drop it," he ordered, and Sherman let go of his shotgun and raised his hands.

"Walk," the hulk ordered.

Sherman obeyed, walking slowly, afraid he might startle the man into squeezing that trigger.

"That's far enough," he ordered, and Sherman stopped.

"Listen," Sherman said, "I lied before when I said I was hunting. I'm looking for—"

"I know what you're looking for," he said. "Tough luck on you." He spat again, then took a mouthful of chewing tobacco from a stained package and started ruminating.

"Have you seen her?"

"Have I seen her?" he laughed derisively. "Sure, I've seen her. My problem is I've seen you, and I got no use for you." He pointed at a shovel lying on the ground next to a tree, a few yards away. "Get busy."

Sherman picked up the shovel and started digging. The soil was soft, moist from the summer rain that had washed over the area just two days before. He kept his eyes on the man, hoping he'd fall asleep or pass out or something, given that he gulped a swig of moonshine every few minutes or so. Nothing seemed to get to him.

He'd dug about a foot of his own grave when he had an idea. When he'd gone to Rapid City that morning, he'd taken all his cash with him. He still had it, as the deal didn't work out as expected. Discreetly, he bent over as if to pick something from the ground and extracted the wad of cash from his pocket.

"Hey, this yours?" he called, holding the cash up in the air and hoping the mountain ogre won't figure out that cash found on the ground should've been moist and dirty, not dry and clean. At least that much the ingested moonshine should do.

Seeing the money, the man sprung to his feet and approached. When he was three feet away, he tucked his gun in his belt and reached for the cash with both his hands, grinning widely and showing stained, crooked teeth. He'd probably never seen that much money before; it was about nine hundred dollars, held together with a metallic clip.

Sherman knew he only had one shot, one fleeting moment before the giant would overcome him. He took a quick breath of air, and, as the man grabbed the cash, Sherman throat punched him with all his strength. The man choked, dropping the cash and taking both his hands to his throat, gasping for air. Sherman didn't waste any time; he grabbed the shovel and smacked him in the head with it, as hard as he could. The man fell to the ground and didn't move. Blood started oozing through his thick, clumped mane of hair into the freshly dug ground.

He rushed to the cabin, calling loudly, "Dolly? Dolly?" desperately looking for the door to the cellar. Only Spot came, and he told him again, "Where's Mom? Let's find Mom."

The dog started to scratch the floor at the edge of a stained carpet, and Sherman pulled it aside, uncovering the cellar door. He lifted it, squinting to see in the pitch-black darkness inside, then took his flashlight and climbed downstairs. Moments later, he climbed back up, carrying Dolly, while Spot circled around them in a frenzy.

He walked outside and set her gently on the grass, then felt for her pulse. It was strong and steady; she was only unconscious. He took her in his arms and started calling her name, caressing her hair, trying to wake her. Spot licked her face enthusiastically and whimpered excitedly when she eventually opened her eyes.

"You came," she whispered. "How did you—"

She froze, and he turned to see what had startled her. The

hulk sat, leaning into his left hand a little wobbly, aiming his gun at Sherman.

"Listen," Sherman said quickly, "You can keep the money, all right?"

"Too late for that," the man replied dryly.

Then he heard a shot and froze, expecting to feel something. Instead, the man fell to the ground, a large blood stain growing on his chest. He looked around and saw Detective Flynn approaching the fallen man cautiously, still holding his gun trained on him.

The cop kicked the man's gun away and felt for a pulse. "He's gone," he said. "Are you all right?" he asked Dolly.

She nodded a few times, wiping tears off her face. "I'll be fine."

"How did he get to you?" Sherman asked his wife. "You see someone like that, and you open the door?"

"He told me you had a car accident at the corner of the street," she said, smiling sadly.

He took her in his arms and held her tight, taking in the joy of finding her alive.

"One thing I don't understand," the cop said, looking at Spot. "This isn't a police dog, right? How did the spaniel track her all the way out here?"

"First," Sherman said, standing with some difficulty, then extending a hand for his wife, "how did *you* find us?"

"We got special permission to begin the search. Then our K9 unit tracked your dog," he replied, "starting from the dog toys scattered all over your yard. See over there? Detective Benson has the dog back in the woods, waiting for me to assess the situation here. But him," he gestured toward Spot with an intrigued smile, "how does a dog like that pull it off?

Dolly smiled and squeezed Sherman's hand.

"He follows her everywhere," Sherman replied with a resigned shrug. "Spot is her dog."

LIES

THE VISITOR

He woke with a start, covered in sweat, his heart racing. He listened intently for a few seconds and heard nothing but the silence of the empty mansion and the whistling wind outside, rattling barren tree branches against the massive windows of the sitting room.

He'd dreamed of her again, and the memory of the nightmare was making him angry. She was dead and buried, and the house was finally regaining its lost dignity, shrouded in the silence and majesty it deserved as the residence of the Earls of Surrey for many generations. Yet she tormented him again, as she did every night, haunting his sleep after she'd finally stopped ruining his days.

His wife... just thinking of the word made him cringe. He chased all thoughts of her away and listened to the howling storm outside, then started a brisk fire in the main fireplace to cheer himself up. The wood had already been put in place by his manservant, and all he had to do was take the flame to the kindling underneath the stack. He had to do that himself, unfortunately. He did his own chores after eight at night, a sacrifice he made for the sake of peace and quiet. His staff was to leave promptly at eight in the evening and not return until six the following morning. Just hearing them move about the house made him livid.

The fire picked up nicely, and he went back to the sofa, where he lay down, exhausted. He didn't feel like going upstairs, to spend the night in his conjugal bed. If it weren't so soon after the funeral, he'd have had the master suite redecorated by now, and all traces of that horrible woman wiped from existence.

He'd almost dozed off again when a sound made him open his eyes. He nearly dismissed it, blaming the tree branches, but the sound repeated, too patterned to be the storm. He shot the massive grandfather clock a quick glance, then went to the door, dragging his slippers and tying his plush robe in a hurry.

He opened the door and quickly stepped backward when the storm sprayed rain all over his face.

"Blimey," he said, then wiped his face and looked at the drenched, shivering stranger on his doorstep. "Who in bloody hell are you, and what do you want?"

"Sorry to bother you," the man replied, his voice shivering in the frigid rain. "My car broke down just up the road, and the moment I took my phone out to call, the rain got to it and it's fried." He showed the Earl of Surrey a phone with a dark screen. "Could I possibly trouble you for the use of your phone?"

George Andrew, Earl of Surrey, was not in the habit of helping people, but that night he welcomed the company of any man, in the hope it would send away the ghost that haunted his dreams. He stepped aside, inviting the stranger to enter.

The man stepped inside and quickly closed the door. He looked at the water pooling at his feet, seeing that it stained the Persian rug. George stared at the man and weighed his options, resisting the urge to throw him back outside in the storm where he'd come from. Instead, he gestured to the guest bathroom.

"Go in there and change; you'll find fresh towels and a bathrobe."

"Thank you very much, sir," the man replied and disappeared into the bathroom. A few minutes later he emerged, his hair still wet, disheveled, and spiky after being toweled vigorously. The stranger hadn't even bothered to run his fingers through that hair of his and didn't care much for appearance, keeping the bathrobe loosely tied and focused more on that dead phone of his. Only one thing could explain such rudeness.

"Are you American?" George asked.

"Yes," the man replied excitedly, grinning widely and showing off some incredible teeth.

Damn the Americans and their bloody teeth, George thought, but then replied, "So was my late wife."

"Oh, really?" the man said, feigning interest so poorly it was pathetic, as he picked up the hall phone to make his call.

George walked into the sitting room, hearing the mumbled words. The man had no education whatsoever, no manners. But his presence sent the ghost away, and there were worse things in life than putting up with his nonexistent manners.

The American soon joined him, asking, "Hey, do you mind if I put my phone on the mantle, over that fire? I'm thinking if it dries out, it might work again."

The Earl of Surrey waved absently, trying to get over the fact that he'd been addressed like a stable boy, with the appellative, "hey."

The visitor spent a few good minutes, making sure his dead phone was in the right position, and leaned the filthy object against a two-hundred-year-old, silver, candlestick holder, then threw himself into an armchair and grinned again.

"Gee, thanks so very much! I know it's late, and I appreciate your hospitality. The towing people said they'll be here in about an hour."

He didn't respond in any way; probably an hour was the most he could stand the stranger, before feeling the urge to strangle him.

"I'm Brian, by the way," the man said. "Brian Miller."

Again, he didn't feel the need to respond, but after a while, he realized he'd better give the man his name or risk being called out like servants. "George," he said.

"You seem upset, George," the man said, giving him a scrutinizing look.

He waved his hand, as if swatting away a fly. "Not your concern, really."

"Maybe I can repay your kindness," the stranger offered. "I'm a therapist, you know, a psychologist. I'd be happy to help; it's the least I can do."

George looked at the man intently, feeling tempted. He was a stranger, soon to be gone from his life forever, and bound by professional standards to absolute secrecy. An anonymous helping hand who probably didn't even know who George was. He stood and poured bourbon in two glasses, then offered one to the man.

"What's your business in the United Kingdom?" he asked.

The man gulped half the bourbon. "No business, just pleasure, if you can call that being stranded in the middle of nowhere. I have a plane to catch tomorrow at noon, going home to Atlanta."

"You've been here a while?"

"No, just this week. No offense, but I'm not coming back. Too much goddamned rain," he said, and shot the rest of the liquor down his throat.

George stayed silent, weighing his options. Maybe talking about some of it would make his nightmares go away. Maybe it would ease his conscience enough to make him sane again.

"It's my wife," he eventually said, not taking his eyes from his glass, now almost completely empty.

"What about her?" Brian asked, in a soft, soothing voice.

"She was American, you know, like you. From Texas. Quite the riot, she was. Katelyne was her name, but we agreed to call her Kate. You know, we had to. People would have... not understood."

Brian listened attentively, and didn't interrupt his flow of troubled thoughts. George checked the time again; it was almost eleven, and this time he almost dreaded the moment the stranger would have to leave.

"Anyway, she's gone now," he added, almost rushing through, but then stopped. How could he dare say more?

"Did you love your wife?" Brian asked, in such a tone of voice that he felt he wasn't going to be judged, no matter what he confessed.

"No," he eventually whispered. "I tried, but I couldn't. Now I feel... guilty."

For a while, the grandfather clock and the cheerful fire made the only sounds he could hear; the howling wind had subsided, and peace engulfed his home again.

"When did she die?" Brian asked.

"Two weeks ago... it's still fresh in my mind."

"I'm very sorry for your loss," he replied gently. "How did she die?"

Silence took over the room again, and this time the crackling fire seemed almost menacing, as if a beast would break out of the fireplace and roar its anger over his sins and burn him alive.

"She fell," he replied, shuddering, unable to shake off the feeling of doom that clung to him like a cold, wet shroud. "In the Beecham ravine; it's south of here."

"You said you tried to love her, but couldn't," Brian said, just a tad above a whisper. "Why is that?"

"She was... rude. Loud, impulsive, out of control. She always said the worst things, and then laughed at them. She listened to music all the time, and it wasn't Bach, if you know what I mean. I tried to educate her, you know, to... stop the embarrassment. She was making a fool of herself, everywhere we went, and of me too. My mother would have been appalled."

"Yet you married her, a young American woman from Texas. What did you expect?" Brian asked, just as gently, but with a hint of humor seeping in his voice, almost sarcastic.

"You're right, I shouldn't have married her," he replied, feeling more confident the stranger would understand and not judge him. "God knows I didn't expect much; she wasn't even a virgin when we... But, you see, I had no choice."

Brian waited patiently for him to continue, and let him gather his thoughts. Before George could share anything else, he had to make sure his biggest secrets were bound to stay secret.

"You're obligated to maintain complete confidentiality of our conversation, by the nature of your profession, are you not?"

"Yes, I am," Brian said. "I'm not licensed to practice in the United Kingdom, but that doesn't change a thing for me. Technically, if you hire me as your therapist, I can't share a word of what we're talking about, not even to the authorities."

George stood and went to his study, then immediately came back and put two hundred pounds in Brian's hand. "Now I've hired you as my therapist; do I have your word?"

"Absolutely," Brian replied.

George took his seat back on the sofa and let himself become engulfed in his thoughts. "I had no choice," he eventually said. "One more year, and I would have been completely bankrupt, bringing centuries of my family's heritage to shame. Having to sell everything, all this," he gestured toward the walls covered in fine Renaissance art. "The first Earl in Great Britain's history to go broke... can you imagine the disgrace?"

Brian nodded calmly, and then asked, "Was she rich, your wife?"

George clenched his fists and gritted his teeth. "God had no good sense of decency when he gave so much wealth to Americans. Oil money, that's what it was. She made her family mad when she came to live here with me, and I was happy they didn't attend the wedding. They were mad at her for marrying me... do you see the irony? And her own brother didn't even come to her funeral. Strange, arrogant people, her family."

"She was in love with you, I reckon?"

"She was," George admitted with a smug smile. "I... made her fall for me. I was courteous and a real gentleman, and I guess she didn't see much of that back in her dust-filled, cowland of a home."

"Was she happy?"

He hesitated and gave Brian a scornful look. This wasn't supposed to be about her; it was about him. His time, his feelings, his guilt. Screw Kate; even now, after she'd been in the ground for two weeks, she managed to take the spotlight away from him.

"She was, when she rode her damn horses, hollering like a madwoman and shooting her guns. But when I asked her to partake in my life and share the things that made me happy, she was bored. She fell asleep at the opera; everyone was talking about it, and the newspapers printed her photo."

"It must have been hard for you, being how important you are. I see that now," Brian said. "But why are you so troubled? Are your finances—"

"No, nothing like that. It's just that I can't sleep at night, not since she died."

Both men were silent for a while. George lit a cigar, filling the room with wisps of bluish smoke.

"When you think of her death, what's the first thing that comes to mind?"

George looked at Brian through the cigar smoke, wondering how much he could trust this man, a stranger who came out of nowhere in the middle of the night, an American, no less.

"I should be relieved, freed, but I don't feel the joy. Now I can marry a properly educated woman, from a good family, who won't embarrass me in public by wearing the wrong attire or telling jokes. Or worse, singing like a tramp while washing her own dishes or chatting with the stable help. Oh, God... can you even imagine?"

Brian didn't reply, but the expression of understanding on his face didn't change.

"I guess you can't really comprehend, being you're an American yourself. But believe me when I tell you, it was an embarrassment to be married to her. That's why I wish I would be able to enjoy my freedom, rather than being haunted by her memory." He paused and studied the incandescent end of his cigar, attentively, as if the details in that miniature hell fire were paramount to his existence. "I feel guilty, that's how I feel. Guilty."

"I understand," Brian said. "She saved you, your family heritage, and you didn't love her. It's normal that you—"

"No, you don't understand anything. I feel guilty because I..." He choked, unable to continue. He couldn't say the words out loud; he wasn't ready yet.

He stood and went to the sidebar to top the bourbon in his glass and took a big swill. He sat again, then closed his eyes and leaned back, ready to abandon himself to the haunting monsters of his conscience.

The sound of the clock seemed loud, now that the fire had burned through most of the wood and was dying quietly. Minutes passed undisturbed, while he kept his eyes closed, inviting his nightmares to return.

"Did you tell anyone else you killed your wife?" Brian asked quietly.

George didn't reply immediately; he kept his eyes closed, but the relief he felt after sharing his burden with that stranger was palpable.

"No," he eventually replied. "I haven't told a soul."

"Did she suffer?"

"No... it was quick."

George felt Brian's strong hands, as he grabbed him and threw him across the room.

"You goddamned bastard," Brain said between gritting teeth. Then George felt a blow to his head and lost consciousness.

When he woke, he was tied to a chair, and Brian was at the door, letting in a few constables and a superintendent, one he knew from fundraisers and political events.

"What's this about?" the superintendent asked, entering the home cautiously.

"You have it all here," the American said, handing over his smartphone. "He killed her, he killed his wife."

"Who are you?"

"Mark Mayfield, her brother."

The American now spoke with a strong Texas accent.

"What were you doing here, Mr. Mayfield?"

The American shot George a glare, then showed the superintendent a folded piece of paper. "My sister sent me this letter, a week before she died."

The superintendent put on gloves and carefully unfolded the letter, then read it aloud.

"Dear Mark," the letter said, "Don't freak out because I'm writing on paper instead of sending the usual email. I believe I'm losing my mind and becoming paranoid, so I'd rather not leave a paper trail, in this case an electronic trail of our conversation. Maybe it's this place, or maybe it's just my overactive imagination, but I think I made a terrible mistake marrying George. I'll hang in here until I can figure out if he loves me or not, but I feel paranoid lately, and yes, I know I've already said that, so in case something were to happen to me, please look in his direction. I'm not saying that it will; I just feel better for sharing my thoughts with you. And no, don't do anything about it; don't come here, guns ablazin', to save your little sis. I can take care of myself, I promise. Love, K."

The superintendent folded the letter and then put it in an evidence bag, after a nod from Mark gave him permission. Then he listened to a piece of the recording on Mark's phone, nodding every few seconds. Finally, he beckoned the two constables.

"Take that man," he said. Then he turned to Mark. "Thank you, Mr. Mayfield. But, if I may ask, why not come to us with the letter?"

"He's an important man in your country. I was afraid you'd look the other way."

"We don't do that here, Mr. Mayfield. Maybe they do it like that in the States, but not here. Not that often, anyway."

The two men shook hands, as the constables took George Andrew, Earl of Surrey, away in cuffs.

"I paid you," George yelled, as they were dragging him away, "I paid you two hundred quid for your silence, you wanker! You said therapists never share secrets!"

"Yeah, about that," Mark said, turning to the superintendent, "you might find in the beginning of that recording that I might have misre—"

"My colleagues are telling me the recording was partially corrupted, Mr. Mayfield. I don't know what you're talking about."

ON THE ICE

It was a long-standing tradition, their annual mountain-climbing trip to Glacier National Park and, despite not feeling anything like rock climbing and sharing a tent with Jeremy, Alan didn't want to break the tradition. Maybe he subconsciously wanted to be alone with the bastard, up there on the ice, with a 7,000-foot freefall at their toes. Maybe, unlike any of the previous years, he secretly hoped his climbing rope would give, and he'd find his death somewhere below.

He climbed lead, on the ice-covered northern versant of Mount Siyeh, which meant he had no safety rope for himself, and he had to stop every foot or so to drive one more piton through the ice into the rock. Twenty feet below him, Jeremy looked up, waiting impatiently for him to drive those pitons into stone, and chatted incessantly, despite the frigid air that nearly froze their lungs every time they inhaled.

"One of the things people appreciate on this mountain is silence," Alan blurted, then looped his rope through the new piton's ring.

"Getting bored here, that's all," Jeremy replied. "Wish I'd brought a book or something. I'm falling asleep."

Always driven, always driving, his pal, Jeremy. He could never stop to enjoy anything, always rushing to achieve. Excellent qualities for a business partner, and that's why the company they'd founded together more than twenty years ago had exceeded every investor's expectations. It had been an excellent run: more than two decades of friendship, of business partnership, of annual ice-capades, as Jeremy liked to call their outings on the glacier, all about to end up there, on the icy top. All soon to be over.

Damned bastard...

He put all his anger into the next couple of hammer strikes, and pieces of dislodged ice and rock fell, some hitting Jeremy's helmet.

"Hey, watch it," he promptly protested, but Alan didn't bother to reply.

Why was he here, anyway, Alan wondered. Why bother, travel for hours by car, then climb this endless chunk of rock and ice, just to... What? What was he planning to say up there, that he couldn't've said back at the office?

A couple more pitons and he reached a small plateau, where they could continue their climb using crampons. He waited on the edge of the plateau for Jeremy to climb the remaining distance, and even before he reached the last of the pitons, his mouth was milling.

"Sure took you long enough," he bickered half-jokingly, "not to mention you're not entertaining at all today. What the hell's wrong with you, and what have you done with my friend, Alan?"

Something swelled Alan's chest, strangling him, despite panting with his mouth open from the last stretch of effort. Then that something took the shape of uncontrollable words that came out of his mouth before he even realized it.

"Ah, save it, Jer. I know you slept with my wife."

Jeremy froze, with one foot in the air, dangling by the rope. "What the hell is wrong with you? What are you talking about?"

Alan stared at the horizon, where the sun was starting its final descent, rushing to leave the world in darkness. He pressed his lips together, then shrugged and looked down at his buddy, an indescribable look of contempt on his face.

"You've always underestimated me, Jeremy. You're doing it again. I would've never opened my mouth, if I wasn't sure about it."

"And I'm telling you, you're wrong," he argued, taking both his hands off the rope to gesticulate, leaving his entire weight entrusted in the figure eight descender. The rope was still looped around his waist, and one foot held firmly on a piton, but he felt and acted overconfident, ballsy, and reckless, in other words, typical Jeremy.

Alan felt disgusted, seeing him act like a teenager caught smoking behind the garden shed. What was he expecting? An immediate confession and a letter of apology? Men lied... women lied too. Yet, somehow, Jeremy's lie made it worse; he'd prefer some honesty for a change, even if it were too damn late.

He crinkled his nose and curled his lip, disgusted. "I have video, Jer."

"You have what?" Jeremy's hands instantly grabbed the rope tightly, but he didn't finish the last couple of yards of climb.

"You heard me."

Jeremy lowered his gaze, then rubbed his face with his gloved hand, as if wiping away something terrible. But, finally, he was quiet for a change. He hung there, stunned, only the wind pushing him around like a puppet on a string.

When he looked up again, he searched Alan's eyes with a steeled look.

"Is this where you cut my rope loose, huh? Is this why we're here, Alan?"

Alan's sad chuckle echoed in the silence of the icy peaks. "Is that what you would've done, Jeremy?"

Jeremy didn't reply. He just stared at Alan and didn't move.

Alan crouched next to the edge, securing his crampons deeply into the icy surface.

"Don't think the thought hasn't crossed my mind," he said, with a wry laugh. "But I can't. I can't and I won't. I've done nothing wrong, and I won't let you turn me into a killer."

Jeremy clenched his jaws, but didn't reply.

Alan held his gaze, then asked, "One thing I need to know, Jeremy. Do you love her?"

Jeremy gave him a long look before speaking. "I've always loved her, you know that. For reasons I can't understand, Elsie chose you, and never looked back. Until..."

The last piton, the one that held the rope safely in place, yielded half an inch, and a loose piece of rock bounced free, rattling against the versant until they couldn't hear it anymore.

"Quit horsing around," Alan said with urgency in his voice, "and get up here, pronto." He tied a safety rope around his waist, then secured it from a piton farther up the slope.

"Is this a trap? Are you screwing with me?" Jeremy asked.

"Stop being an idiot, and get up here already," Alan shouted, and this time Jeremy listened.

He climbed as quickly as he could, quickly putting his feet on pitons, holding on to the rope with both hands. Then the last piton gave another bit, and both men gasped.

"Damn it to hell, Jer; take my hand!" Alan shouted, leaning forward from the edge, as far as he could without slipping off.

Jeremy reached out and grabbed Alan's hand, the moment the last piton gave another inch, and scraped the versant with his feet, desperately looking for some footing to help him climb over the edge. Alan pulled hard, but his glove started to slip.

"Come on, reach, grab anything," he shouted, and Jeremy flailed with his other arm, trying to grasp at something.

Jeremy finally found a small crest he could grab onto and started pulling himself up, while Alan pulled him by the back of his harness. When he finally felt his weight firmly supported by the icy slope, he let himself stop squirming and breathed.

"Thanks," Jeremy said, then coughed, exhausted.

Alan replayed Jeremy's words in his mind, over and over again. *Elsie chose you, and never looked back. Until...* He often wondered why Elsie had chosen him. Jeremy was taller, better built, and probably smarter than Alan was. He had a way with women, knowing exactly what to say and when, how to make them feel special. Yet he'd never married, and not for lack of enthusiastic options. Maybe he *was* telling the truth; maybe he loved Elsie and she loved him, no matter how it tore Alan inside to admit it.

He stood up and moved farther away from the edge, then reached down and extended his hand, helping Jeremy get up on his feet.

"I'll get out of the way, Jeremy. I'll—"

"What the hell are you talking about?"

"Elsie."

"Don't be an idiot," Jeremy replied. "She loves you. With me, it never mattered. It was an accident, a mistake."

Alan stared at Jeremy, wondering what made him lie again.

"You were away in Japan, closing the deal with the manufacturer. You hadn't called in days. I saw her wandering about aimlessly at the mall, and I took her to dinner. She was sad, she missed you, and you'd barely been there for the past few months. She feared you were having an affair. I took her home afterwards, and... I'm sorry, Alan. I am."

"Instead of telling her I was working my ass off to get that deal signed, you slept with her?" He felt rage coming up his throat, dragging a wave of bile with it.

"I told her, I swear I did. But she started crying, she told me about your date night, and how you always took her out to eat at the Great Wall of China on the first of the month, celebrating your first date. She told me you'd stood her up for months, then she was all tearful, standing there... I took her in my arms. But it never meant anything, not for her, anyway. She didn't take my calls the following days, never replied to my e-mails. She kicked me to the curb, and I deserved it."

Alan stood silently, feeling the bitter wind whipping his frozen cheeks, and wondered where his happiness vanished. How was it possible that twenty years of marriage, of friendship, could be taken away in a matter of seconds? A backstabbing friend, a cheating wife, the two most important people in his life had turned against him and left him hollow, broken, and bleeding.

Then he realized whose fault it really was.

When Alan got home the next evening, he rushed inside the house, looking for Elsie. She was reading on the sofa, in front of a lit fireplace, but she stood quickly, pale, and let him hug her without saying a word. Then she sniffled quietly.

"Alan, we have to talk. There's something I need to tell you."

"Yes, I know," he replied, hugging her tightly and caressing her hair. "You're craving Chinese, and I'm taking you tonight. Happy belated date night, sweetheart. Let's go, the Great Wall of China is waiting for us."

"But, Alan—" she started to say, pulling herself away from his embrace.

He covered her mouth with a long kiss and folded her in his arms again. "Nothing you could tell me, sweetheart, would change how much I love you."

GAMES

He shook his head in disbelief, watching his wife clear the table, taking trick after trick with a devious smile. She'd bid an impossible contract, of six spades no less, but somehow managed to deliver it. Now all she had to do was be a good sport about it, and not rub it in their opponents' faces.

That would be the day. His wife was out for blood. Again.

When she played bridge, she completely forgot that Mark and Nicole were their lifelong friends, and that their game at the Nassau Bay Country Club was a monthly recurrence. Bridge partners were hard to find, especially good ones, but Jennifer didn't seem to care, not when she sat across from Nicole, wielding her tongue like a machete and taking no prisoners.

He dreaded the day Mark and Nicole would pass on the monthly game; at this rate, it was bound to happen, eventually. Their monthly tradition went way back, probably fifteen years, since Mark had his heart attack and took early retirement.

They had an entire routine to their card games. At first, the two of them teamed up against Mark and Nicole. Then the women teamed up against the men. That was the rubber he liked the most, because his partner was a rational, calm individual who liked to bid by the book and followed all the rules. Finally, Jennifer teamed up with Mark, while he got to play across from Nicole. That wasn't too bad either; if he were to ignore his wife's murderous looks, every time he won a contract.

This time it didn't seem they were going to reach that third pairing. His wife, an otherwise classy and sophisticated woman in her late fifties, was being a complete ass. What made it worse, she was also winning.

Mark dealt the cards and Nicole opened. "One heart," she whispered, and immediately shot Jennifer a guilty glance.

Jim counted his cards. He had enough points to open, but decided against bidding. He couldn't lose with the points he held, but he decided it was safer to sabotage Mark and himself by playing poorly, than by bidding against Jennifer. Mark would understand.

"Pass," Jim said.

"Two spades," Jennifer said calmly.

Nicole frowned. Mark passed, and silence ensued while Nicole counted her points again.

"Three hearts," she said, then put her cards on the table facedown.

"Three spades," Jennifer countered, not even waiting for Jim to enter his bid. At that point in the bidding war, the only thing he could say was "pass." Or "double," but he wasn't crazy, to openly challenge his wife's bid.

Nicole shuffled her cards again, left to right, and then back. She arranged them a little, and then drew a deep breath. "I'm sorry, Jen, I have to... four hearts."

"Bitch," Jennifer mumbled, and Jim kicked her promptly under the table. The woman was losing it, pushing it too far.

"It drives me crazy," Jennifer said, reviewing her cards angrily. "Where the hell are the points? She obviously doesn't have them, and you two have passed. So, all right, six hearts, if you want hearts all that badly, sweetie," she hissed toward Nicole.

Mark and Nicole passed in a hurry.

"Pass," Jim added. "But I got to tell you, hon, this is wrong. You're playing with your trump cards on the table. That's a rookie mistake."

"I know how to play, dearie," Jennifer replied, calmer than he'd expected. "I think I've already proven that. But no way in hell am I going to lay *my* cards here, in the open, and play dead, while the bitch over there plays with two men, not one. Do you see what I'm sayin'?"

Her Texas accent grew stronger when she got mad and started speaking slowly, not faster, like other human beings did when they got angry. Nope, not Jennifer. She turned calm and cold as ice, because, in her own words, "Revenge is best served cold."

Nicole turned pale and bit her lip. But maybe the evening could still be salvaged.

"Yes, dear, you're right." Here he was, uttering the most hated four words in all male population, yet the words were guaranteed to bring instant peace, armistice in all marital battles.

"Well, get ready for the game, then," Jennifer said. "I need a minute."

She walked toward the ladies' room with her head held high, swaying her hips a little, and taking her time. Nicole stood, and the two men also stood, out of chivalry, although Mark was ogling the waiter with a desperate glance. His bourbon was probably going to be a double.

"I'll… go after her," Nicole said, "just to make sure she's all right."

She trotted quickly across the game room toward the ladies' room and entered without hesitation.

Jennifer sat in front of the mirror, powdering her nose and playing, at times, with a long curl of her blonde hair. That curl had escaped the blue satin ribbon that held her hair together in a loose ponytail.

Nicole leaned against the marble counter and smiled. "How do you do it? You don't show any roots. You have to have some grays in there."

Jennifer tilted her head and smiled at her through the mirror. "I do highlights, not bleach. It tricks the eye. There are plenty of grays in there, unfortunately, only you can't see them anymore."

Nicole nodded, then, after a few seconds, added in an assertive tone. "Don't call me a bitch anymore, okay?"

"Seriously? Aren't you forgetting you slept with my husband?" Jennifer chuckled. "I can call you whatever the hell I want."

"Well, aren't *you* forgetting something?" Nicole pushed back, throwing her wavy chestnut hair over her shoulder. "Who started it? Huh?"

"What do you mean?" Jennifer replied, feigning ignorance so poorly she almost laughed at herself.

"You slept with *my* husband first. I only slept with Jim once, to get even. You started this; don't you ever forget it."

Jennifer held Nicole's gaze in the mirror for a long time, and then eventually cracked a coquettish smile. "I did, didn't I?"

Nicole nodded a few times, and then burst into laughter. "So, we've established, you're the bitch."

"I am," Jennifer admitted, and stood, admiring her slim figure in the wall-sized mirror. "I used to be hot back then. Cute and sexy. I had this tight little ass, and tiny breasts, and my skin was—"

"I hated your ass," Nicole said, "I still do. Mine's not that firm anymore."

"I hated your boobs. What were they, a D-cup?"

"Uh-huh, but that's a pain over time, you know. You're better off now, trust me."

"Okay, I'll give you that, but I remember back then, when you shoved those beauties under Jim's nose, he didn't stand a chance. That night, he didn't sleep. He kept saying he couldn't breathe. Yeah... I bet."

The two women hugged each other sideways, still looking in the mirror.

"So, what's it going to cost them this time?" Nicole asked.

"There's a new restaurant in Houston; it's ultra-high end. They say the filet mignon is worth dying for."

"And let them get away with dinner? That's not enough for this month. Remember, Mark doesn't know that I know. We can work this to the bone, even if it's been almost twenty years."

"All right, bitch, what do you want this time?" Jennifer asked, laughing.

"I think it's time for a cruise in the Caribbean, don't you think? We need some ocean tan."

Jennifer thought for a second. "Let's do that, but I want dinner too. I'm craving myself some filet mignon."

They pecked each other's cheeks, then walked out of the ladies' room, slowly, as two Army generals who'd just signed a volatile truce.

Out on the terrace, Jim and Mark were almost done with their cigars, and their bourbon glasses were already empty.

"What do you think it's going to be this time?" Mark asked.

"Who knows? Whatever keeps them happy, right?" Jim patted Mark on the shoulder, a couple of times.

"Yeah..." Mark sighed. "If we were so stupid, what can I say?"

"Nah... it's more fun like this. It doesn't feel like we're getting old; it feels like yesterday we fooled around and got caught. At our age, women are fighting over us, clawing at each other's eyes. Beautiful women too! That's a privilege... That's youth, my friend, forever youth."

LAST WILL

The moment she stepped onto the Amtrak train platform, Tracy's smile widened, showing two rows of still perfectly white teeth. She tilted her head back, closed her eyes, and inhaled deeply, feeling the cold, fresh mountain air enter her lungs and the warm touch of the sun on her face. It felt just as she remembered; it felt like home.

She gave the white-trimmed peaks of Big Mountain another loving look, then started pulling her wheelie on the platform toward the street exit. The same two tracks rolled into Glacier Falls Depot, but the train station looked nice, probably recently renovated. She frowned a little, trying to remember if it was the same building she remembered, but she couldn't be sure. That night, more than twenty years ago, didn't hold many fond memories; none, really.

She passed the two cabbies who were trying to get her attention and continued south, letting her eyes wander from one storefront to another. Almost unchanged... strange how time almost leaves no marks in a place like Glacier Falls, Montana. No high-rise buildings like in Chicago, no traffic jams, no honking horns, and no screeching tires in the suffocating summer heat. No, just blue skies, so blue it didn't seem real, and a postcard-worthy landscape, frozen in time, although cars had kept up with the ages. If it weren't for the latest Ford truck model she saw in the Saloon parking lot, she would've thought she'd somehow traveled through time.

"Well, if it isn't Tracy Tillman Hemsworth!" a woman's cheerful voice erupted right next to Tracy, startling her. Then the woman grabbed her arms firmly and hugged her, then smooched both her cheeks. "My dear, you look lovely!"

Tracy took a small step back and racked her brain, trying to remember. Ahh… her grammar school teacher, Mrs. Galek. Tracy didn't remember her as the kindest of people, but she'd always been fair to Tracy, although a bit prone to feed on her family's newsworthy tidbits and fuel the town's gossip mill with endless yarns of mostly imaginary tales.

"Good to see you, Mrs. Galek," she said, smiling. It felt good to be recognized, greeted warmly. Not something she could expect upon her arrival at the family estate, so she let her heart bask in the warmth of that furtive interaction.

"I'm happy to see you, although I am very sad about the circumstances. Your grandmother… she will be missed."

The thought of Grannie's passing brought instant tears to her eyes, and she looked sideways, trying to focus her mind on something that would help keep her emotions under control.

"So sorry, my dear," Mrs. Galek whispered, squeezing her hand. "Do you think they'll be civil about it?"

Tracy looked at Mrs. Galek with inquisitive eyes.

"Well, rumor has it that your aunt, Patricia Tillman Gaye, will not let you set foot on the property. That's what she's been telling people, and she hasn't been discreet about it."

Tracy rolled her eyes. Her aunt and uncle, the people who'd wanted nothing less than to chase her away from her family's home, only a few months after her parents had died. It was after a fight with Patricia that she found herself running all the way to the Amtrak station with a broken heart and barely enough money clutched in the palm of her hand to cover the ticket to Chicago, leaving behind everything she'd ever known and loved.

"I'll be fine, Mrs. Galek. I'm not that scaredy girl anymore, and I have the right to be here. I was invited by the executor of the estate."

"Yes, I heard that, but do you think they'll let you attend the funeral tomorrow?"

Tracy chuckled bitterly. "Let them try to stop me."

"That's the girl I remember," Mrs. Galek said, putting a wide grin on her face and suddenly eager to leave, probably rushing to spread the news about what was bound to be the town's biggest scandal since she'd left, twenty-three years ago.

A couple of smooches later, Mrs. Galek headed straight for the Café, while Tracy resumed walking, backtracking her steps from that night long ago. That's why she'd chosen to travel by train, instead of booking a flight to Spokane and driving a rental car to the mansion. It was probably going to be the last time she'd visit Glacier Falls, and she wanted to remember everything, every tear she'd cried that night, out of breath, freezing in the fierce January snowsquall, running away. How could Patricia have been her mother's sister? How could someone so vicious have been Grannie's daughter?

A car pulled to the curb next to Tracy, but she barely noticed it, lost in her thoughts and haunted by memories she'd thought forgotten. A man rushed to her and stopped right in front of her. His blue-green eyes glinted with anger, and the furrow crossing his brow underscored his menacing look.

"How dare you show your face here, you slut," he shouted, impervious to the discreet glances thrown by passersby. "You're here to embarrass us, huh? Bring our good name to shame? Is that it?"

She held her ground firmly and locked her eyes with his in an unspoken clench of wills. "Get out of my way, please," she replied calmly. Her uncle's rage fits were not new to her.

"Do you know what this will do to Patricia?" he shouted again, refusing to move.

"Don't know and don't care," she replied firmly.

"Don't you dare cross that property line, you hear me? I'll have people with guns waiting for you. You set foot on that land, you're dead."

She smiled, then rolled her wheelie past him and continued down the street. A quick glance in the store window at her right revealed the reflection of Charles Tillman Gaye, frozen in place right there on the sidewalk, his clenched fists close to his chest, and his face disfigured by anger. She almost smiled, and then continued her way at the same steady pace.

A few minutes later, the hotel receptionist where she'd made her reservation apologized profusely and mentioned something about being overbooked, last-minute emergencies, and, "We're terribly sorry, but there's nothing we can do. You'll have to find lodging elsewhere."

So that was the way the game was played in Glacier Falls, Montana. No one dared to stand against the Tillman Gayes. How very reassuring. It was also understandable, considering they were one of the wealthiest families in the state and owned most of the town's businesses. Anyone who wanted to work had to work for them, directly or indirectly. The hotel, although a major chain's franchise, was owned and operated locally, and she understood its problem. Suddenly, the town didn't feel like the home she remembered from before her parents died. More and more, it felt like the frozen, stormy night that she'd left.

Tracy walked out of the hotel and hailed a cab, then gave the cabbie an address. As she did, she noticed his eyebrows pop up, and she smiled crookedly.

"That address is in the Blackfeet Indian Reservation now, ma'am. I know you've been gone—"

"It was in the reservation even before I was gone," Tracy replied calmly. Was there anyone in that town who didn't know who she was? Probably not.

~~~~~

When she knocked on the door, she didn't know what to expect from Blackbird, or if he was still alive. She felt small, unwanted, waiting on that porch in the dimming sunlight, feeling her heart beating loudly against her chest.

The door opened with a long creak of aged wood and rusty hinges, and she looked at the man holding it open. She recognized him at first, but then she didn't anymore. Time had not been kind to him. His once proud stature was gone, and his hands shook a little. His face, burned by wind and sun, was covered in myriad lines. But his dark eyes lit up when he recognized her, and he smiled, then uttered something in his language.

She smiled back. "What was that?" she asked.

"Your Blackfeet name," he said, "Nuttah."

"I didn't know I had one," she replied, blushing. Blackbird had said more than that one word in his native tongue, but she didn't insist. "What does it mean?"

"It means my heart."

"Ah," she replied quietly, as tears welled up in her eyes.

"Come in," he said, then made room for her to enter the small home.

She stepped inside and inhaled the familiar scent of incense, then looked around the room. Nothing had changed, not a single item had been moved or replaced in more than two decades. It was as if life had stood still since the day she left. She followed Blackbird to the backyard and sat on a rocking chair, not minding the dust on it, and waited for him to light his cigarette.

"I was hoping you'd stop by," he said. "I wasn't sure you would."

"I... wasn't sure either," she admitted, looking at the stunning view of the mountain at sunset. "I didn't know if you wanted to see me again. It's my fault—"

"It's not," Blackbird cut her off, almost shouting. "Never say that. You're a kind, loving soul. It wasn't you. It was them."

She sat quietly, rocking almost imperceptibly, watching Blackbird's internal turmoil reflecting on his smoke-engulfed features.

"They took my son and robbed him of his life. They took your life too. No one else but them. Ahanu is with the spirits now, and he knows I speak the truth."

A tear rolled down her cheek when she heard his name spoken out loud, the name she'd been whispering in her thoughts for all those years.

"Will I see her?" Blackbird asked.

"Tomorrow, right after the service. She's flying in for that," Tracy replied, knowing exactly whom Blackbird was talking about. "I didn't want her to take the brunt of their... hate."

He nodded slowly, and released another puff of smoke from his lungs.

"She has his eyes, you know," Tracy added, then bit her lip to keep the sobs locked in her chest. "She's beautiful, and smart, and laughs a lot, just like he used to."

Tracy pulled out her smartphone and showed Blackbird a photo. "Her name is Kimi."

Blackbird took his eyes off the phone's screen to shoot her a quick, inquisitive glance.

"No, not a coincidence," she said, smiling sadly. "It's what Ahanu wanted to name her. Our little secret," she added, referring to the name's meaning in Blackfeet dialect.

"He knew?" Blackbird stood abruptly, sending the rocking chair into a frantic back-and-forth, then leaned against the porch rail, looking into the distance.

"Yes," she whispered. "I was almost three months pregnant when I—"

Her voice trailed off, hesitant to say the words again. Memories of that terrible day came rushing in, and she pressed her hand on her chest, feeling the hollow inside open wider, threatening to swallow her. She forced herself to breathe and continued to stare in the distance at the snow-topped mountains, now shaded in deep crimson against a dark blue sky.

"My mother was called Kimi," Blackbird eventually said, and lit another cigarette. "She and Charlotte were best friends when they were little."

Hearing her grandmother's name spoken out loud brought a chill to her bones, a reminder that she was gone, the last connection she held dear with the place that had taken so much from her.

"They used to play together, right under that tree," Blackbird said softly, pointing a trembling, crooked finger toward a cherry tree. "They'd climb up and down that tree all day long and eat the fruit as soon as it ripened. Then they grew up, and went their separate ways, but their friendship never wavered. It didn't matter what people said, not to Charlotte, not to Mother."

Tracy shuddered, feeling the evening chill grab her heart and twist it with frozen fingers. Blackfeet people never spoke the name of the deceased, afraid that they'd be called back to earth instead of finding their way to the spirit world.

As if he read her mind, Blackbird turned halfway toward her and said, "She's here, you know. Her spirit never left, waiting for you. You've come, and now she can rest."

Tracy covered her mouth with her hand and swallowed a sob. Only a whimper came out.

"Nituna, Nuttah," Blackbird whispered, then touched her shoulder with a warm, gentle hand.

"What does it mean?" Tracy asked, and sniffled quietly.

"It means, 'my daughter, my heart.'"

She took his hand and pressed her cheek against it, letting her tears flow freely.

"She didn't look it, but I think your grandmother was Siksika people," Blackbird said, using the native name for one of the four original Blackfeet tribes. "She understood our ways, and the spirits spoke to her." He hummed a few notes of a native song filled with sadness, then stopped and took another drag of smoke. "She tried, you know. She fought for him."

Tracy looked up at him, surprised.

"Early next morning, she was at the sheriff's office with her lawyers, ready to testify he'd done nothing wrong, but it was too late. He was gone."

"That sheriff, he shouldn't have listened—"

"It wasn't his fault, Nuttah. He did his job, nothing more. It was them, your aunt and uncle, and that deputy who worked for the sheriff. That deputy died a year later, mauled by a bear. Some Siksika say that was my son's angry spirit that took his life."

Another wave of suffocating anger swelled Tracy's heart. Her own family, Patricia and Charles, who were supposed to care for her well-being, had torn their lives apart. They'd threatened to put her into a private clinic to have an abortion, so that "the shame would be gone." She'd ran out of that house, not knowing they'd go after Ahanu next, making false accusations, and having him thrown in jail. He died that night, her kindred spirit, the love of her life, all alone in a cold, dark cell, at the hands of a misguided, corrupt cop. By the time she found out what happened, it was too late.

Tracy had blamed herself for everything that had happened that night. If she had gone to see Grannie instead of running away, he would still be alive. If she'd just stayed that night, to face the storm, no matter how bad it would have been. Many things would have been different if she'd just... stayed.

"They put her in the small house," Blackbird continued, referring to Grannie Charlotte. "Many years ago. The jackals wanted the big house for themselves and had her moved to the small guest house, near the main gate."

"I know," Tracy whispered between clenched jaws. "Then they had her declared incompetent and all the estate placed in a trust."

"The bobcat isn't to blame for his bloodlust," Blackbird said quietly. "It's his nature."

They fell quiet for a few long minutes, then Blackbird went inside for a few seconds and returned with a blanket he draped around her shoulders, then took his seat in the other rocking chair, next to her.

"Do you have a good life, Nuttah?" he asked after a while.

Her mind had wandered far away, to the sunny days of her youth, to the mountain paths she'd climbed, hand in hand with her secret fiancé, dreaming about their future together, choosing names for their baby.

"Kimi makes it all worthwhile," she replied eventually. "She's all I have."

"No husband? Boyfriend?" Blackbird's voice was gentle, understanding.

"No," she said. "I couldn't. He was my soul mate."

Silence engulfed the covered patio for a few minutes, as the last remainders of the day disappeared from the sky, leaving the moon shining brightly against the star-filled sky. She hadn't seen a sky like that, not in any other place.

When he spoke again, Blackbird's voice was hardened. "What will you do tomorrow?"

"I'll go to the funeral. That's what I came here to do, whether they like it or not. I'm meeting Kimi at the Café, and then we'll drive to the cemetery together."

"I would come too," he said, "but the sheriff told me not to. Be careful tomorrow. Be the fox that runs and lives, not the bear that stays and dies."

The following morning, she woke up bright and early and drove Blackbird's old truck straight to the sheriff's office. By the time she cut the engine and put the parking brake on, the sheriff was waiting for her in the doorway, with his thumbs stuck in his belt loops. He wasn't smiling, but he tilted his head a bit, as she approached, and took his right index finger halfway to the rim of his hat.

"Miss Tillman Hemsworth," he greeted her in a somber voice. "I heard you were in town."

"Yes, Sheriff, I am. I need your help to make sure my grandmother's funeral will be a peaceful event."

"Then maybe you shouldn't attend, ma'am. If you don't, it will be a peaceful event for sure."

Tracy bit her lip and swallowed the Chicago cusswords she'd picked up since she moved there. Instead, she looked him straight in the eye and took a step closer to him.

"Twenty-three years ago, you didn't do the right thing, and you know it. I'm sure regret has haunted you since, because you don't strike me as the type of fellow who lacks conscience. Why don't you do the right thing today, when you have a chance?"

"Ma'am, I know the estate executor from Spokane put you on the list, but I still think you should limit your presence to that event."

"Sheriff, you killed a man twenty-three years ago. You killed him, just as if you'd pulled the trigger yourself."

The sheriff adjusted his belt buckle and shifted uncomfortably from one foot to the other. "The family has expressed—"

"I'm family too, Sheriff. I'm family who'll call the state troopers in a jiffy if you're not able to do your job here, or if you feel overwhelmed and need some assistance."

"No, ma'am, that won't be necessary. I'll bring a couple of deputies. No need for more."

She turned around and left, allowing herself to breathe after the tension of the exchange. She'd thrown the state troopers into the conversation as a last resort, not even knowing if that strategy could work.

Tracy next drove to the Café, where a silver rental sedan was the only car in the parking lot. Kimi's silhouette was visible through the Café window, hunched over her smartphone and sipping from a tall cup. She rushed inside and hugged her tightly, not willing to let her go, until she protested.

"Mom!"

"Okay, okay," she replied, feeling a little emotional. "Let's go."

They drove both cars, and stopped by Blackbird's place to drop off his truck, then continued in the rental sedan all the way to the cemetery.

"Mom, this place is… so weird!" Kimi said. "It's like stuck in time or something."

She chuckled. "It is, isn't it?"

They pulled into the cemetery parking lot and got out of the car, just as a black Mercedes pulled in right next to them. Tracy grabbed Kimi's hand, urging her to rush, but Kimi had a mind of her own.

"C'mon, Mom, don't freak out. I'll be fine, and you'll be fine too."

Kimi adjusted her lipstick and got out of the car, as a woman in her sixties watched the two of them with disapproving eyes.

"I heard you were coming here today, and couldn't believe it," the woman said.

"Mrs. Frost," Tracy acknowledged her coldly.

"Why, you haven't heard of people attending funerals before?" Kimi snapped.

"And this would be your... half-breed?" Mrs. Frost asked, the venomous undertones in her voice unmistakable. Tracy felt her blood boil.

"Oh, yeah, that's me," Kimi replied, before Tracy could open her mouth. "I guess that makes you the overdressed, sanctimonious bitch, right? Nice to meet you!"

Glints of rage sparkled in all three women's eyes, but Tracy drew in a deep breath and reached for Kimi's hand. "Let's go," she whispered.

Mrs. Frost had been bitter ever since her son Daniel was courting Tracy, intently yet dispassionately, probably on a mission from his mother to marry into the Tillman family fortune. The fact that he'd failed to conquer Tracy's heart was bad enough, but he'd lost the battle in favor of a redskin, a boy with no fortune and no future. That insult had made Mrs. Frost livid, and livid she had been ever since.

"To think I welcomed you in my home," she shouted, as they were leaving. "A waitress, that's what you are. My son told me he couldn't eat at your restaurant in Chicago."

Tracy stopped in her tracks. Dan Frost had been at her restaurant? When?

"What are you talking about?"

"Huh! Like you don't know. He was there a few years ago, and thought he'd look you up, to see how you were. But no, he couldn't even get a table there. What kind of restaurant is that, all booked ahead for months? They must work you like slaves, huh?"

Kimi scoffed and rolled her eyes, then muttered under her breath, "What a certifiable idiot!"

Tracy's smile tugged at the corner of her lips. "Did he mention my name or ask to see me?"

"Um, no, I don't think so. What's a waitress going to do, right?"

"Woman, stop embarrassing yourself," Kimi blurted, "she owns the place."

"What? That fancy restaurant? Chogan's Place? No..."

"Yeah, well, you can eat your heart out, old bat," Kimi replied dryly. "She owns the Chicago Chogan's Place, the New York one, and the San Francisco one too. Not bad for a pregnant girl from Glacier Falls, Montana, huh?"

"Kimi," Tracy said quietly, urging her daughter to tie up that loose tongue of hers, and Kimi threw her a quick look and stopped talking.

They resumed their walk toward the cemetery gates, as Mrs. Frost had turned pale, her ridiculous hat crooked on her head, and her mouth gaped open. Then they entered the cemetery escorted somewhat discreetly by the sheriff and one of his deputies.

The service was beautiful, although riddled with smirks and glares from the family and hateful gazes thrown in her daughter's direction. Kimi stared defiantly at everyone who dared look at her the wrong way, and soon Tracy stopped worrying about Kimi and started to say her own goodbyes to Grannie. When she looked up again, she saw Blackbird standing right there by her side. The rest of the attendees had stiffened up even more, their faces devoid of any expression, other than the utmost outrage.

As soon as the service ended, Patricia stood and coldly announced they were pushing forward the reading of the will, and all those invited to participate were asked to proceed to the main residence. There was no need to further delay that, in the interest of everyone's time. Tracy almost smiled, hearing how desperate Patricia was to see her and Kimi gone.

When they arrived at the Tillman residence, they were surprised to see they'd been assigned front-row seats in a crowded room, filled with Grannie's friends, neighbors, and distant family. Not a word was spoken between the two women and the rest of the family; only loaded looks, averted eyes, and whispered comments behind their backs. Nothing they didn't expect.

The executor of the estate appeared and took his position at the center of the room, introduced by the family attorney. He was a tall, thin, and balding man, approaching his sixties with dignity and an increasing bend in his back, not uncommon in aging, tall people. He must have been more than six foot four in his younger days and still towered over the gathering.

He cleared his throat and everyone fell silent, waiting for him to start.

"Good afternoon, everyone. We are gathered here today for the reading of the last will and testament of Charlotte Tillman, dated this past June, on the fifth."

Patricia fidgeted and raised her hand. "There must be some mistake. My mother was declared mentally incompetent almost fourteen years ago, and the entire estate has been placed in a trust. We were named her primary legal guardians in a court of law." She sounded irritated, almost suffocating with anger, as she spoke the words that brought murmurs in the audience. Apparently, not everyone present was aware of what Patricia and Charles had been up to.

The executor shuffled though some papers, then nodded. "That is true. However, Mrs. Tillman had that decision reversed a few months later, after undergoing a panel examination of her mental faculties. She was deemed completely capable and her full rights restored."

"Why weren't we told? Don't the courts notify people of such things?" Patricia's pitch climbed higher with every word.

"On her special request, the court granted Mrs. Tillman the right to keep the ruling a secret. She had reasons to believe there was malicious intent behind the initiative to have her declared mentally incompetent, and she didn't want to live in fear for her life. The court granted the request for confidentiality that my firm handled on her behalf."

Gasps filled the room, and whispers rose like waves in the ocean before a storm. The sheriff took a few steps closer, leaving the doorsill he'd been leaning against and approaching Patricia's seat.

Patricia covered her gaping mouth with her hand and sat silently, watching the executor with bewildered eyes.

"But three times a year she was being admitted to the psychiatric hospital for treatment," Charles insisted. "I drove her there myself, every time."

"In one door, out the other," the executor said coldly. "Mrs. Tillman had become a significant benefactor of that hospital, and the staff agreed to assist her with this innocent charade."

"With what money?" Patricia snapped. "She didn't have anything left. Everything was placed in trust."

The audience gasped again, reacting to the knowledge that the founder of Tillman Enterprises, Charlotte Tillman, had been stripped of her entire fortune. The glares started to concentrate on Patricia and Charles, and the whispers rose to the point where the executor had to call the room to order.

As soon as the gathering fell quiet again, the executor pressed a button on a remote and the 55-inch TV came to life, displaying a slideshow of photos taken throughout the years. Most of them showed Charlotte visiting a variety of tourist attractions, sometimes alone, sometimes with Tracy, and other times with both Tracy and Kimi. There she was, overlooking the Golden Gate Bridge in San Francisco, smiling widely and holding Kimi's hand when the girl couldn't have been a day older than five. Visiting Chicago's Aquarium. Hiking at Yellowstone, staring at Old Faithful, and throwing pebbles in the Grand Prismatic Spring with a mischievous smile on her lips. Signing their names in the golden sand of Miami Beach.

Looking at the Niagara Falls lightshow after dark, from the Canadian side.

"She had a passport?" Patricia reacted, but no one bothered to reply.

Tracy wiped a tear from the corner of her eye, seeing all those memories the three of them had made during the years. Tracy never understood why she'd let Patricia and Charles get away with their scam for so many years, but she respected Grannie's wishes nevertheless.

"And now, the reading of the actual will, signed, as I previously stated, this past June, on the fifth."

He proceeded naming one by one almost everyone present, for whom Charlotte had left something—a valuable work of art, a memento of their friendship, a souvenir. Then the executor said Patricia's name, and the gathering froze, holding their collective breath.

"To Patricia and her husband, Charles, I leave one of life's most important lessons, that they somehow missed," he read the words written by Charlotte herself. "As Patricia's mother, I consider myself to blame for what she has become; I have failed as a parent because my only surviving daughter has no respect for any values other than monetary ones. All these years I have waited for my daughter to come to her senses and change her ways, but it was all in vain. As such, I use this last opportunity to teach her what I have failed to, as her mother. Hence, my daughter, Patricia, and her husband, Charles, will not receive anything of monetary value from the family estate."

All heads turned to stare at the two of them as they sat huddled together, clasping hands, pale, distraught.

"Furthermore, all the funds that the two of them have been skimming throughout the years from the trust and squirreling away in the Caymans have been seized and returned to the family bank accounts. Finally, there's something about consequences that Patricia needs to learn. Many years ago, she wrongfully accused a young man of stealing an emerald ring, and Charles supported her accusation. Consequently, the young man, my great-granddaughter's father, was arrested and later that day died while in custody, before I could intervene. The ring my daughter had claimed was stolen is hidden in her bedroom dresser, taped under her sock drawer. I only hope the statute of limitations for their crime has not run its course yet."

"There's no statute of limitation for murder in the state of Montana," the sheriff intervened.

The executor cleared his throat again and took a sip of water before continuing. "To Blackbird's family, I owe an immense debt that I can never repay. Our family was responsible for the loss of their son, and there isn't anything anyone can do to repair that. I only hope they can find a way to forgive me. I place in the hands of my friend, Blackbird, the deed to the family farm, with taxes paid in advance for the next fifty years, for him to manage or use at his discretion."

Tracy turned around, looking for Blackbird. He hadn't said a word about attending the will reading, but there he was, standing in the doorway, escorted by a deputy. He wore the full regalia, including the feathered headdress, and, as his name was read, he started humming the same sad song she'd heard him intonate the night before.

"Finally, the balance of the estate will go to my granddaughter, Tracy. You have proven your worth as a businesswoman, and I know the empire I've built will thrive in your capable hands. You have given me joy these past years, and for that, I can never thank you enough. And you have given me Kimi, the light of my life. This house will be hers, to hold and cherish as the place where both her bloodlines intersected and created the beautiful spirit that she is."

The executor closed the file folder and took off his glasses, while people started to murmur, as they made their way toward the door. Tracy turned and looked for Blackbird, and there he was, by the door, standing with dignity as bewildered people passed by him. She walked over to him and clasped his hand.

"This is your granddaughter, Kimi."

Behind them, Tracy could hear the sheriff reading Patricia and Charles their rights, but she didn't care to look. She watched with mesmerized eyes as Kimi and Blackbird connected, their souls instantly touching each other.

"I've roasted some buffalo this morning," Blackbird said. "Will you honor my table?"

"Are you kidding me?" Kimi replied. "I'm starving!"

The three of them locked arms and headed for the main entrance, walking slowly, letting other people rush by. Mrs. Frost walked past, but then stopped and turned around, shaking her head slowly.

"I thought you were broke," she said. "I thought you were a nobody, but you bankrolled all her travels, her donations, all of that? You must be something else, and I'm sorry I misjudged you. That Chogan's Place must be doing really well."

"It is," she said, smiling crookedly.

"Chogan's Place?" Blackbird intervened. "That's the name of your restaurant? Do you know what that means?"

"Yes, I do. It means Blackbird's Place," Tracy replied, smiling. "No, not a coincidence."

OPHELIA

J oy rushed to the minivan, breathing shallow, afraid to invite the frozen air deep inside her lungs. Each new breath whirled mist around her face, but she paid little attention to the swirls that used to bring giggles when she was a child. Now she was an adult, running errands as fast as she possibly could and making sure everything was perfect for her three-year-old's birthday party later that afternoon.

She pulled the minivan's side door open just enough to drop the grocery bags she was carrying, throwing them inside without concern. Two six-packs of Bud Light and some salty snacks for the dads weren't exactly eggs; the cans couldn't break. And if one of them should have his beer foam up when he popped the top, well, tough luck; let the mighty men of Trout River, Iowa, run errands in the freezing cold next time. She'd have rather spent her day at home, with the fireplace crackling, hanging decorations and consoling little Matthew, who wanted his birthday moved to July, like his sister's, so he could have the inflatable bounce house and a water slide.

She slammed the door shut, then climbed behind the wheel and started the engine without wasting another second. With the heater cranked to the max, she rubbed her hands together in front of the vents to warm her frozen fingers. The weight of the bags had dug white lines into her flesh, slow to disappear. She should've worn gloves.

She breathed, letting the warm air fill her lungs, then touched up her lipstick, pressing her lips together afterwards to smooth their luscious surface. She crinkled her nose, noticing an acrid smell coming from the vent, but didn't think much of it, although she couldn't identify the odor. That minivan was a battlefield of childrearing, and she never seemed to keep it properly cleaned.

"One of these days," she mumbled, her version of a promise. "But not today. Definitely not today."

She had one more errand left, to pick up Matt's cake. The bakery was less than a mile away, then she could head back to the farm and start getting the food ready before everyone showed up.

And rehearse some more lines with her anxious, oh-so-teenage daughter, Taylor. Again. And again.

What idiot had come up with the idea to select *Hamlet* as a children's school play? Not the modernized, abridged version, but the original one. Of course, it was Mr. Whitaker, the pretentious braggart, none other than her daughter's English teacher and a consistent pain in the collective faculty's rear, an old snob who didn't realize the times had changed and those kids were better off learning how to survive, how to master job interviews and the fight to make ends meet, not perform *Hamlet*.

And fifteen-year-old Taylor had put up quite the fight for the privilege of playing Ophelia's part; she hadn't given up until the cast list revealed her name on the shiny billboard in bold letters, right next to the famous character of Shakespeare's play. Ever since she'd secured the role, she'd been rehearsing. In front of the mirror. On camera or off. In the kitchen. With full costume or jeans and a T-shirt. Late at night, barging tearfully into her parents' bedroom, script in hand, begging Joy to read lines with her.

Damn Shakespeare, screw Ophelia, and damn that old coot, Whitaker, and the day he chose to become a teacher, Joy thought, yawning until her jaw cracked. She hadn't fallen asleep until two in the morning, and the first thing that had come to her dreams when she finally got some slumber was a stupid line her daughter couldn't get right.

"Fare you well, my love!" Taylor had said, her voice

trembling with well-acted tears.

"It's my *dove*, baby," she'd muttered, struggling to keep her eyes open. "My *dove*."

"Mom!" she'd reacted, quick to slam the script on the table and angrily pace the room. "You're supposed to read the next line, not interrupt me every time." She'd propped one hand on her hip. "Can't believe she calls him dove. It's stupid."

Joy smiled to herself in the rearview mirror and shifted into drive. After all, reading Shakespeare with her daughter and running errands for Matt's birthday were not bad problems to have, and she was grateful for the life she had.

She slowly set the minivan in motion, careful not to slide on the thick ice and brush against the car parked beside her, then sped up as she joined the thin traffic of the early Saturday afternoon. By the time she turned on route A52, there was no other car in sight, just empty road covered in fresh snow, meandering under heavy tree branches, an idyllic drive.

She was about to call Logan, her husband, when she sensed something moving in the back of the minivan. She took her foot off the gas and looked in the rearview mirror, then froze.

A strange man grinned at her from the third row, his teeth crooked and stained. "Hello, my dear," he said in a raspy voice, thickened by years of cheap smokes and moonshine. When he spoke, a renewed wave of the acrid smell drifted her way, nauseating.

Her heart thumping in her chest, she pulled to the side of the road, slammed on the brakes, and turned to look at him, her jaw slack and her hands shaking badly.

"Who are you?" she managed, wondering why she hadn't noticed him when she'd put the groceries in the car. He now sat on the third row of seats, right next to Matt's child seat. He'd probably waited for her crouched on the floor, a spider ready for its prey. "What do you want?"

He eased himself closer, sliding between the two seats on

the second row, and sat on the right side. Joy slowly turned her body toward the back seat and watched anxiously as he ran one grimy hand through his disheveled, greasy hair, strands falling on his sweaty forehead, then pulled the other hand from the pocket of his thin jacket.

Joy's petrified gaze followed his move, then focused on the gun he was holding, casually aimed at her. Her breath caught, strangled by agonizing fear.

Panicked thoughts rushed through her brain, looking for a way out. Could she risk trying to call someone? Could she take a chance and move, ever so slightly? She slid her left hand into her pocket, as slowly as she could, trying to reach her phone. If she could only trigger a 911 call, that would probably be enough. The dispatcher would know what to do, especially when the operator, who was Matt's godmother, recognized her number.

Half-turned toward the stranger, Joy kept her eyes on the gun barrel and asked, "What do you want?" while her fingers found the phone in her pocket and turned off the sound. Frenzied, she tried to recall what triggered the emergency call. It was one tap, then a second on the screen, then lower left. Or was it lower right? She wished she'd paid more attention.

"You think you're so damn smart," the man snapped, his stained smile instantly replaced by a scowl. "Give me that phone," he demanded, prodding her with the gun.

She shook her head, whimpering, but he prodded her again.

"Okay, okay," she said, then took out the phone and handed it to him. The call hadn't initiated; the screen was locked and dark.

He grabbed it and bounced it in his hand for a moment, thinking. Then he opened the window and threw it out.

The damn 911 call hadn't happened.

But they'd start looking for her really soon, she encouraged herself, the moment she didn't show up to fix Matt's birthday dinner or read lines with Taylor. Then both the sheriff and his deputy would roam the streets of the small town looking for her.

They'd find her phone, out there in the bushes by the side of route A52. They'd know something was wrong. They'd bring a K9 unit, maybe even a chopper, if they couldn't find her.

There was still hope. Unless the man pulled the trigger, and then she'd never see her family again.

Unwanted tears burned her eyes and tightened the knot in her throat. She whimpered, trying to hold them back. "I—I have money, you know," she blurted, digging through her right pocket for her wallet. She remembered having about thirty dollars in there, but maybe that would be enough, and he'd let her go.

The man sucked his teeth. "Huh... you got money, you say?"

"Yeah, I do," she nodded, sending her hair in loose strands across her face. "Here, take all I've got," she offered, handing him the cash.

"Sure, why not?" he laughed, grabbing the cash and shoving it in his pocket. "I'll take your money."

She hoped he would just leave, but no, he didn't seem like he was going to. Laughter died on his face, replaced by a hatred-filled scowl.

"Drive," he ordered, poking her shoulder with the gun.

He stood and moved to the front passenger seat, then fastened his seatbelt, the gun still pointed at her.

She quickly glanced at him, her heart pounding, her breath shattered in panicked gasps of air.

"Drive already," he ordered, aiming the gun at the side of her neck. She flinched when the cold metal touched her skin.

"Wh—where to?" she asked, her voice trembling badly.

"Home," he replied coldly, caressing her cheek with the barrel of his gun. "Weren't you going home, my dear?"

She felt the blood drain from her face, leaving nothing behind but sheer panic.

"What, you weren't going to invite me to Matt's birthday party?" he asked, his voice loaded with hatred and something else she feared to understand. "Tsk, tsk," he laughed, "how rude of you. But don't worry, I'll teach you some manners."

She held her breath, her foot hesitant above the pedal. She looked desperately into the rearview mirror, hoping someone would drive by, so she could ram into their car and create an incident, enough to immobilize the minivan and get someone to call the sheriff's office. No one was there, only the thickening mist under a gloomy winter sky, sieving snowflakes without stopping.

"Drive," he hissed, bringing his mouth close to her ear and punctuating his demand with another shove of the gun's cold barrel against her neck.

She started driving on the slippery road, thinking, pacing her breathing, pressing her left hand against her chest to summon some reason and disperse the panic, while her right hand tightly gripped the steering wheel.

The man knew a lot about her, about Matt, about the family's plans for the afternoon. Yet he seemed to be a complete stranger, someone who'd been living on the streets by all appearances. She didn't know who he was, and he wasn't willing to share. But if he knew about Matt's birthday, he must've known where she lived.

Then why hadn't he come to the house, gun in hand, to do whatever he had in his sick mind to do?

Easy, she thought. He would've risked finding Logan there, maybe their friend Ed too. It didn't make sense to break and enter, and risk being shot, when he could be driven straight into the family garage.

If he knew where they lived, he knew how to get there. She only had to drive ten miles before she would turn on 133rd

Avenue, heading home. It was the only road leading to the farmhouse, weaving between picturesque, wooded hills and snow-covered patches of farmland.

"Step on it," he ordered, "ain't got all day."

She threw a quick glance toward him, and, in a split second, imagined what it meant arriving at the house with that man. What if Logan wasn't home yet? Her kids... they'd be sitting ducks. She couldn't risk their lives.

Even if that meant she wasn't going to see them again.

She took one deep breath of air, feeling surprisingly at peace.

Then she floored it and threw the man a crooked smile.

"Fare you well, my dove," she muttered, thinking of Ophelia and the impossible choice that had driven her to take her own life.

"What?" he reacted, staring at her with lust-filled eyes that made her sick to her stomach.

She grabbed the wheel with both hands. "There's a lot you don't know about me, Mr., um, I'm afraid I don't know your name."

"You don't need to know it," he said.

She watched her speedometer increasing to about sixty on the slippery road. Snow was starting to accumulate, the existing salt on the road insufficient to keep up with the new, constant supply. "I've had a rough patch lately, Mr. whatever-your-name-is." She sniffled, inhaled, then gave the minivan more gas. She didn't have much time left.

"So, what's that to me, huh?" he reacted, then spat on the floor, between his worn-out boots covered in mud.

"Well, I'm ready to die, sir," she said, feeling calmer as she stated the words she'd started to accept. She'd sooner slam the minivan against a tree than take that man to her house, to her children. "Are *you* ready to die?" she asked, turning toward him with a dark smile and watching his reaction.

He seemed a little paler, and his scowl had vanished. Then his jaw clenched, muscles dancing under the grimy, stubbly face. He put the gun against her temple. "I'll kill you right here, bitch. Don't fuck with me."

She floored it. Then she threw him another glance. "Go for it."

His hand faltered.

"You're doing me a favor," she added, stalling for time, unsure what to do next. "I only have three months left to live, Mr. whatever. I'd have to do it anyway." She smiled widely, thinking of Ophelia again and how rehearsing that endless play with her daughter had made it easy for her to lie. It wasn't really lying; it was acting. "I'd rather take you with me when I go."

"You fucking bitch!" he bellowed. "Don't you tell me that! You do as I say, or—"

"Or what? You'll kill me?"

She laughed wholeheartedly, feeling a little high on adrenaline. Soon she'd slam the minivan into a tree. Her turn was approaching, and the road home was covered in gravel. No way she could go seventy on gravel. But for now, for another three or four miles, she held all the cards.

She held her breath, knowing it had to happen, knowing it was coming. Fresh tears blurred her vision as she recalled the last time she'd seen her kids, her husband. Their laughs, their voices, their touches.

Then she remembered a story Logan had told her, about how distressed drivers used to ask for help many years ago, before smartphones and the 911 dispatch. They used to fly a handkerchief out the window of their car, so everyone would know they had an emergency.

She didn't have one, but she wore a white scarf.

The minivan swerved as it drove over a patch of ice, and she barely kept it on the road. Nervous, she lowered the window on her side.

"I'm a little hot, Mr. whatever. Aren't you a little hot?" she asked, grinning his way. "Impending death does that to people. It's the rush of adrenaline."

He was holding on to the door handle, muttering oaths under his stinking breath.

"You're damn crazy," he replied. "Just like that husband of yours."

Slowly, without him noticing, she untied her scarf and let the tasseled endings fly out the window, pulled by the wind.

She had two miles to go, until reaching the turn, and one chance. If only a car would pass by, heading into town.

She saw headlights approaching and knew it was her only shot. She positioned herself better, pushing her back against the seat, loosening more and more of her scarf. It now flew and waved in the wind, visible from a distance, unable to miss. When the time was right, she'd let go of it.

She rehearsed the steps in her mind. First, she'd let the scarf fly out just as the other driver passed, so they'd see it. Then she'd release the seatbelt button for her unwanted passenger. She'd quickly drop the speed to about forty with a slam on the brakes, and ram the first available tree head on. At forty, maybe she'd live. Maybe. He probably wouldn't, and that made it all worthwhile.

When the approaching car was at the right distance, she let go of the scarf, and the wind picked it up, tossed it a couple of times, then let it dance; it landed right in front of the other car. "Oops," she muttered, seeing her passenger riled by her actions.

Her fingers found the passenger seat belt buckle with ease, and she covered the click of releasing it with a feigned cough. The man completely missed it, busy swearing loudly when he saw the other car slowing, red brake lights bright in the fading light. Then she braked, planning to reduce speed just a little before hitting a tree.

She hadn't considered the ice. In snow, she might've still had a chance.

The minivan swerved violently, then rolled over a couple of times before hitting a light pole and spinning into a tree. By then, Joy was unconscious.

The frigid air brought her back to her senses. She felt dizzy, confused, then started remembering what had happened. A pang of pain in her left leg reminded her she was alive.

She couldn't move. She panicked for a moment, then opened her eyes and realized the road was flooded in red and blue lights from the emergency crews. That meant Logan was probably near. She focused her blurry vision, then her weary mind.

What was left of the minivan was wrapped around a large fir tree, and paramedics were loading the man on a stretcher. He was gone, it seemed, since the EMS technician was zipping a black body bag. She realized she was strapped on a stretcher, ready to be loaded into an ambulance.

Sheesh, I hope I don't have to share another ride with him, she thought. Then she felt Logan's warm hand squeeze hers.

"Hey, baby," he said. "You're safe now, and you'll be all right."

A tear rolled down her cheek while she couldn't find her words.

"Quite the adventure today, huh?" the sheriff's voice thundered. Ed Byrd was always loud, no matter the circumstances. He seemed grim, tense.

"I—I can explain," she replied. "I, um, he—"

"No need," Ed interrupted. "The piece of scum you dealt with was wanted for murder, two warrants in two states."

"Why... us?" she asked, feeling weak and shaky as the adrenaline left her body.

"Logan put his sorry ass behind bars a few years ago," Ed replied, patting his deputy on the shoulder. "I guess he came looking for payback." He turned and gave the body bag a long stare. "Serves him right for going after a cop's wife."

MURDER

NOISY CREEK

He shoved the young man into the holding cell and locked the door behind him, then stomped his feet to get rid of the snow that still clung to his boots. He ran his gloved hands against the sleeves of his parka, and more snow fell on the stained floor.

The detainee, a nineteen-year-old by the name of Corey Williams, sat on the splintered, wooden bench without saying a word, his eyes riveted on the black iron bars that took away his freedom. He hadn't said a single word after he was picked up by the sheriff's deputy, resigned to sit wherever he was told with his hands buried inside his pockets.

Mark took off his parka and went to the adjacent room, where Sheriff Dunn chewed on a toothpick with a miserable look on his face. Since he'd quit smoking he had turned into a wretched, sometimes angry man, the sad, empty shell of the feisty, lively lawman he once was. Yeah... smoking might've been bad for his lungs, but had done wonders for the sheriff, and Mark knew he probably wasn't going to see the boss he once knew emerge back to life. Not anytime soon.

The sheriff had packed on a few pounds too, constantly munching on pretzels and chips to keep the urge to light up at bay. Each day at about three in the afternoon, several empty packs of junk food littered the wire mesh trash can, and the sheriff routinely moved on to pencil ends and toothpicks, while his mood turned another degree of sour.

Mark sighed, taking all that in with a single, casual look, and stepped inside his boss's office.

"I got Williams," he announced, taking his hat off and running his hand through his sweat-clumped hair. "He didn't resist."

Dunn threw him a jaded look. "Got anything on him?"

Mark stopped in front of Dunn's weathered desk and propped his hands on his hips.

"That's exactly it, boss. We got nothing. There's no body, no blood, no reason to suspect Williams, other than what Archie's mother said."

"That's good enough for me," Dunn replied coldly, staring at Mark with a steely gaze.

Mark took a small step back without realizing it.

"With all due respect, sir, I understand you have a relationship with Mrs. Moore, but her son could be anywhere in the world by now. She didn't have any information; she just doesn't care much for Williams and she pointed her finger at that boy."

The sheriff spat the munched toothpick into the trash with a flick of his tongue then promptly extracted a fresh one from the pack.

"You've seen Archie," Dunn said morosely, "d'you think that kid had it in him to run away?"

Almost resigned, Mark lowered his head, staring at his scuffed boots while he recalled Archie's image. A mellow, eighteen-year-old kid whose only brush-ups with the law had been joyriding his mom's car when he was fourteen, and drinking beer at his best friend Corey's sixteenth birthday party. Pale and freckled, with kind, hazel eyes and a mop of unruly hair that had been unruly all his life despite his mother's best efforts, Archie wasn't the driven type who'd one day pick up and leave Teton County in search for a better life. No, he'd always seemed like the type who, once born in Wyoming, was going to live his entire life there, working on horse farms and hiking the Tetons. Everything was simple and straightforward about Archie Moore.

Only he'd vanished two days ago, and Mrs. Moore swore that the last time she'd seen her son was when he went fishing for trout in Noisy Creek, with Corey Williams.

Corey Williams… he was different. He could pitch a baseball faster and more accurately than anyone he'd ever seen. If Corey'd been born someplace else, he'd probably be playing the major leagues by now, making shitloads of money. He had a rebel streak, that boy, and a stern look of defiance in his eyes whenever he interacted with authority. Surprisingly, he'd never been in any trouble with the law, but Mark was willing to bet a good hundred bucks that was because Corey was smarter than Archie. People like Corey rarely got caught, no matter what they did.

But to jump from that to suspicion of murder was a bit too much for Mark to stomach, even if his boss insisted.

"Okay," Mark said, "I'll give you that, Archie wasn't runaway material, but that boy, Corey, is his best friend. Why kill him? And why assume Archie is dead in the first place?"

Dunn raised his chubby hands in the air. "Why not go in there with him and find out? It wouldn't be the first time in history when friends turn on each other, maybe for a fine piece of tail like Josephine. They both have the hots for that girl, don't they?"

"For the pastor's daughter? Yeah, that's the rumor I'm hearing."

He turned and left, heading for the holding cell. Maybe Dunn had a point; there was something off about Corey Williams, even if he couldn't put his finger on it. That morning, when he'd picked up Corey, the boy didn't even ask why, and that's always a dead giveaway.

Mark unlocked the cell and grabbed Corey's arm, leading him to the small interview room. That's what the ADA called it whenever she visited with them and that was less than once a year. Good thing she wasn't there to grill them for dragging in a kid without a warrant, without even bothering to read him his rights.

Yet Corey seemed scared of something other than Mark, shooting quick glances sideways and examining every inch of the corridor that led to the interview room. Once the door closed and they were seated at the small metallic table, Corey seemed relieved and breathed with ease. His eyes still searched the one-way mirror on the wall with a frown of concern, but Mark could tell that whatever he was afraid of wasn't close anymore. Strange.

Mark weighed his options and decided not to ask him directly what worried him. Instead, he asked about Archie.

"Tell me when's the last time you saw Archie."

Corey shifted in his seat and wiped his nose with a quick pass against his sleeve.

"Um, day before yesterday. We went fishing."

"Noisy Creek?"

"Uh-huh."

"Tell me about Noisy Creek."

Corey shot him an inquisitive look, as if doubting his sanity.

"Um, they call it that 'cause it's real noisy. You have to yell to cover it. It's 'cause of the big boulders and water running over them and stuff, and the waterfall too."

"You kidding me, right?" Mark asked, ruffling his bushy eyebrows, and trying to determine whether the kid was messing with him.

"That's what you asked, man, sorry." He leaned back against his chair and looked down.

Mark let out an aggravated groan. Yeah, that was exactly what he'd asked him.

"Tell me what happened the day before yesterday, all of it. Start with when you woke up."

Corey shifted in his seat again, then shot the one-way mirror a worried look.

"It was Sunday, so we went to church first."

"I didn't peg you for churchgoing," Mark said, his voice loaded with sarcasm.

"I'm not," Corey admitted with a shy smile. "It's for a girl. We both went."

"Josephine?"

Corey nodded, and his smile bloomed against his will, while his cheeks colored a little.

"You both like that girl," Mark said. "How's that working out for the two of you?"

He shrugged. "Fine, I guess."

"Fine? You never argued over her?"

"Uh-uh."

"Which one of you is dating her?"

He chuckled, keeping his gaze lowered and his shoulders hunched. "She hasn't decided yet."

"Ah, I see," Mark replied. "So, you both threw your names in the hat, and she gets to pick? No hard feelings?"

"No hard feelings... Archie's like my brother."

As he said the words, he looked briefly at Mark, with a hint of sadness in his blue eyes. That sadness was real.

"So, where is Archie?"

Corey shook his head slowly. "I don't know."

"What happened after fishing? Did you catch any?"

"We caught a couple."

"Then you walked back home? Is that it?"

"No..." Corey said, shooting worried glances at the one-way mirror again. "He disappeared. I already told you that."

"How could he disappear without you noticing? Wasn't he standing right next to you?"

"Um, he was... but he disappeared."

"Did you look for him?"

"Uh-huh," he replied, nodding at the same time, and looking at Mark with pleading eyes. "I swear I did. He wasn't anywhere."

Mark let a long, frustrated breath of air escape his chest.

"How wide is Noisy Creek where you two were fishing?"

Corey looked at him for a long moment before replying, while concern ridged his forehead.

"About fifteen feet or so. We like to go right next to the falls, up where the water pools. Plenty trout there."

"But the waterfall's screaming there, you can barely hear a noise."

"Yeah."

Mark stopped short of asking why they'd choose a place where they couldn't hear each other talking. Then he realized the two probably didn't have all that much to talk about.

"Did Archie fall in the water, Corey?"

He shrugged again, then shook his head. "I don't—um, no, he didn't."

Mark nodded once, thinking. There was definitely something that young man wasn't sharing, but he wasn't getting any guilty vibes from him. Only anguish, whenever he looked at that one-way mirror.

"Did you guys drink?"

"Uh-uh, no, sir," he replied, a little too fast.

"Two young men, fishing by themselves in the middle of nowhere, and you want me to believe no one brought a six-pack along for the ride?"

He shrugged, still keeping his head lowered. "It was cold," he mumbled in way of an apology.

"Liquor, then? Some moonshine to keep you warm?"

Corey stayed silent for a long moment, staring at his boots. Then he flickered a quick gaze at the mirror, then whispered, "Just a little, I swear."

"Ah..." Mark replied, "just a little. What's a little to you?"

"A couple of inches on the bottom of Dad's bottle, not a drop more. We barely felt it."

"Both of you drank?"

"Yes, sir."

Corey started tapping his foot quietly against the floor, probably nervous, impatient to get away from there, from Mark and his questions. Mark knew he was getting close to whatever that kid had to hide.

"Okay, Corey, then what happened?"

He shrugged and lowered his head again, and didn't say another word, no matter how many times Mark asked.

What could've gone wrong with the two boys? No one had ever seen them arguing, and the entire town knew them as best friends since grammar school. Not troublemakers, not angels either, just normal teenagers.

Mark leaned against the wall and closed his eyes, visualizing the two on the creek's southern bank, bracing the cold and having the entire landscape to themselves, baiting their weighted hooks with minnows and throwing them over and over again, because trout in winter are lazy, stay glued to the bottom, and won't move much to take the bait.

He visualized them passing the bottle back and forth between them, laughing and chatting loudly, almost covered by the noise of the nearby falls. Then they caught one, a handsome river trout, and had no trouble reeling it in. Then what happened?

The scene froze in his mind, while he forced his imagination to take over and move the players around. It was cold, they drank a bit, stomped the snow along the bank to keep their feet warm. He'd seen where they stood, later that day when he took the K9s up there and started the search for Archie. But the dogs were confused, and they stopped whimpering at the creek's edge. Then he took them to a crossing point and to the northern bank, hoping they'd pick up

Archie's scent on the other side, but they couldn't. All evidence led to the conclusion Archie had fallen in the creek.

He'd seen Corey's bootprints marking the pristine snow as he ran downstream, then entered the water. Corey had told Mark he was trying to find Archie, in the event that he'd fallen in the water, but he came out empty, freezing to death in his wet clothing, against the brisk mountain wind. He barely made it home alive that day, and his mother had to wrap his toes in sour cabbage leaves to keep frostbite at bay.

But then, if Archie had fallen in the water, why didn't Corey just say so? Why was he afraid and what was he afraid of? He opened his eyes and studied the young man; there wasn't guilt in his demeanor, just sadness, resignation, and that anguish he couldn't place. What if there were a third person at the creek with them? Mark and the other deputies had examined the entire bank for footprints, but everyone wore the same kind of boots around there, and size eleven was common to many. As if to spite him, another snowsquall had blown in and added a couple of inches more overnight, building snow drifts and hiding the potential third person's tracks.

He closed his eyes again, and this time his imagination didn't disappoint. Two kids, in the bitter cold, drinking, fishing... then what?

"You don't know what happened to Archie because you weren't there," Mark said, more of a statement than a question.

A tear rolled on Corey's cheek, but he didn't raise his head and didn't speak a word.

"You had to relieve yourself, didn't you?" he asked, remembering the icy, yellowish stain that colored the snow next to a tree trunk, a few yards away.

Corey nodded slightly.

"Tell me what you saw," Mark insisted, in an encouraging whisper, touching the young man's shoulder, and pulling a chair to sit next to him.

There it was, another quick, worried gaze shot toward the mirror.

"Keep your back turned to that window and your voice low," Mark said, bringing his head closer to Corey's, "and only I will hear what you say. It's just me here, and you know you can trust me."

Corey looked at him with tear-filled eyes, an inquisitive look that sought reassurance. "But Sheriff Dunn doesn't like me and he'll try to pin anything on me to make himself look good."

"You've known me for years, kid," Mark said, "Whatever you're afraid of, I can protect you." He allowed him a quick moment, then continued. "Tell me what happened to your best friend."

"He's dead," the young man whispered, wringing his hands together.

"Who killed him?" Mark asked, keeping his voice just as low and wrapping his arm around Corey's shoulders.

Corey looked at him for a quick moment, then said, "A cop."

Mark frowned and distanced himself from the young man. "Say what?"

"No, not one like you," Corey quickly said, still whispering, then shot another quick glance at the one-way mirror.

Mark frowned. "What do you mean, not like me?"

Corey gestured toward Mark. "He wore a blue parka. Yours is green."

"You mean a city cop?"

Corey nodded, staring at his boots some more. "From Jackson. I recognized the badge."

Mark leaned back against his chair and cupped his chin in the palm of his hand. Why would a Jackson cop haul it all the way to Noisy Creek to kill an irrelevant kid? It made no sense at all.

"Why?" Mark asked in a whisper, leaning toward Corey.

This time, Corey didn't shrug. His shoulders tensed and rose, as if trying to protect his skinny neck. "We... fucked it up, man. We didn't mean to."

Mark pursed his lips. "Tell me."

"Last Sunday we went hiking on the Jack Pine Creek banks, toward Granite Springs." He sniffled and ran his sleeve against his nose again. "We found a cabin... his cabin."

"And?" Mark asked, his frown deepening. Just because two kids came by someone's cabin didn't justify killing them.

"We thought it was deserted; it looked like it was about to fall apart. We went inside to warm up and we, um, found meth."

"What, like, drugs?"

"Yeah, that cop cooked meth in there. We didn't think he was inside. We heard a noise... We wanted to run. I was faster, but Archie... he saw Archie. He never saw me."

"So, you got away?" Mark asked, encouraging Corey to continue, but making a note of his use of past tense when talking about that cop.

"Yeah... he fired a couple of shots but missed Archie. It was almost dark. We ran like crazy out of there, didn't stop until we got home. I thought we got away with it."

"Why not tell us, Corey? Why not tell me?"

"You shittin' me? Point my finger at a cop? And what if you were all in on it together? I don't want to die. Archie didn't want to die." His voice was ridden with emotion, but still a whisper.

"Then what happened, the day before yesterday?"

"Um, just like you said. I went to take a leak, only a few yards away. Then I heard a shot."

His face scrunched up, and he ran his hand nervously across his features, as if trying to straighten it up. His fingers were trembling slightly, but he didn't seem to notice.

"What did you do?" Mark asked in a quiet voice.

"I hid behind the tree trunk then peeked to see. Archie was gone, but the cop was there, looking toward the waterfall from the edge of the creek."

Mark waited patiently, but nothing more came out of Corey's mouth.

"And then?" he asked.

"He put his gun into his holster and watched the water for a minute or two. He looked over his shoulder once or twice, but didn't see me." Corey flashed a worried glance at Mark, then lowered his voice even more. "Then he fell into the creek."

Mark's eyebrows shot up. "Just like that, he fell?"

Corey lowered his head and turned his face away from Mark. "He must've slipped on the ice, or something. Maybe on a boulder. They were slick from all that ice."

Mark leaned against the back rest and closed his eyes briefly. He could see Corey taking a leak, startled by the gunshot. He could visualize the cop's back, arranging his parka after holstering his weapon. But he couldn't see him just slip and fall into the creek. Not by himself, no.

He looked at Corey with a scrutinizing gaze.

"If we hike all the way up there and we don't find Archie's body with a slug in him, you're in a world of trouble, kid. Not to mention, we better find that meth cabin, or else."

"I'll take you," Corey offered in a heartbeat. "I swear it's there. Both of them are there," he blurted, then averted his eyes quickly.

"What?" Mark reacted, pushing back from the table in a long, angry screech of metal chair legs against concrete. "You saw him fall and you let him die in there?"

"I, um, ran as quickly as I could, but when I got there he wasn't moving. I checked on Archie, but he was dead. Shot in the head," he added, his voice trailing off, loaded with sorrow.

Something still wasn't adding up. They'd been by the creek the day before, with K9s and all, and no one saw anything in that water.

"Where the hell are you saying they fell, Corey? I didn't see them."

"That's 'cause you don't know the water up there," Corey replied calmly, not raising his eyes from the floor. "The waterfall is strong, and it twists and swirls in that pool at the bottom, taking everything it carries behind the curtain, against the rocks. That's where they are."

Mark stood and leaned against the wall, closing his eyes again and trying to recall the waterfall, the pool at the bottom, the layout of the steep ravine. The falls were halfway iced over, and if water had grabbed the two men's bodies and dragged them against the back wall, they couldn't've seen them. The K9s couldn't've smelled them. Corey could be telling the truth.

With one exception though.

He remembered Corey playing ball last summer, grabbing that baseball and feeling it against his hands, twisting it in his palm as if to mold it into the right shape, then throwing it toward the hitter with incredible speed and precision. The crowd cheered every time he pitched a ball.

That memory faded away, replaced by an image of Corey, slack-jawed and scared out of his mind, grabbing a small rock from the ground and weighing it in his palm. Then, effortlessly, that rock flying toward the cop and hitting him in the back of his head. Within a split second, he would've been gone, not realizing what hit him, already unconscious, carried away by the angry creek toward the 30-foot waterfall.

Mark opened his eyes and stared Corey in the eye. "He just fell, huh?"

Corey turned pale, but managed to speak, his lips dry and almost white. "I swear, that's what happened."

Mark tilted his head and pressed his lips together. There wasn't anything more to be said and done, not before he could see with his own eyes the two bodies. Not before he could match the slug pulled out of Archie's head with that cop's holstered weapon.

A few hours later, Sheriff Dunn, chewing noisily on a toothpick with a jackhammer motion, had assembled a small team on snowmobiles on the southern bank of the creek, ready to go into the icy water and pull out the bodies, if they could find them. Mark waited on the bank, studying the layout, the iced-over boulders at the edge of the creek, taking in the landscape detail by detail.

Loud yelling covered the waterfall's noise, and he turned to see the men dragging two bodies toward the shore, then loading them onto the sleds attached to the snowmobiles. Then the caravan moved on, but Mark stayed behind and climbed to the place where the boys had been fishing. He took one of the small, red flags and stuck it in the snow, to mark the place where he remembered the footprints were the densest.

He walked into the woods a few yards, recalling the yellowish spot of urine, where Corey had stood while Archie had been shot. Mark could see the waterfall clearly from there. The red flag was in a direct, unobstructed view. Corey was telling the truth, at least about that. He would've been able to see the cop from where he stood, holstering his weapon.

Mark crouched and ran his gloved hand through the snow, moving it to the side to uncover the boulders on the ground. Twigs, brown, fallen leaves, and shiny, round boulders covered the earth. Some boulders were large, but others were small, about the size of a baseball. He took one into his hands and weighed it, as if getting ready to pitch it toward the creekbank. For him, it would've been hard to hit anyone from that distance. For Corey? Piece of cake.

"What's on your mind?" Dunn asked, startling him.

Mark turned around slowly, sliding the boulder inside the pocket of his parka.

"Nothing much... just checking the details in the kid's statement." Mark cleared his voice. It almost never happened that he lied to his boss. In fact, he couldn't think of another time that he'd done that. "I thought you'd gone back with the rest of them."

"I knew that cop," Dunn said, pausing to switch the toothpick to the other side of his mouth. "I could've sworn he was clean. I guess we've all got bad habits; we never really know people."

"No, we don't," Mark replied, slowly extracting his hand from his pocket. "Forensics will confirm everything we need to know."

"The cabin was right where the Williams kid said, property in the cop's name, loaded with meth lab paraphernalia," Dunn replied morosely.

"Oh, I didn't know that," Mark replied, patting his pocket to make sure the Velcro tape held it shut.

"What about the Williams brat?" Dunn asked. "You mean to tell me he just stood and watched?"

Mark nodded a couple of times, his frozen lips pressed tightly together.

"Yeah... what else could he do? He was just a kid against a dirty cop with a gun, in the middle of nowhere. He's lucky to be alive."

UNFORGETTABLE

Detective Saul Klein peered through the one-way mirror and frowned, then turned to his partner.

"Got the wrong suspect in there, Grant. Am I missing something?"

Kristy Grant smiled cryptically and tilted her head just a little, the way she did when she followed a hunch.

"Let me have an hour with her in the sweatbox, and you might yet be surprised."

"Why are you looking at this woman? She's not the black widow; her daughter is."

They both watched the fifty-seven-year-old woman, who sat calmly on the metal chair, her hands folded neatly in her lap, and her face devoid of any emotion other than a hint of irritation. Her auburn hair, styled to perfection in a layered bob, gave her complexion a pale appearance, or maybe it was the fluorescent lights reflected against the off-white walls.

"Call it a hunch," Kristy replied, unwilling to explain more. She and Saul Klein had been partners for almost seven years, since she'd made detective in LAPD's Hollywood Station. He accepted a woman as his partner reluctantly, but not any less elegantly. Initially, he'd been circumspect about her abilities as an investigator but never a chauvinist nor a pig, and she was still grateful for that. A few months later, he'd become her mentor. Fast forward to the present, she still felt like a rookie, being coached by a seasoned LAPD cop.

"C'mon, Grant, give," he insisted, looking at her for a second, then back at the woman in the interrogation room.

She sighed, a quick burst of air leaving her lungs under pressure. "It was a smirk."

"A what?"

"Remember yesterday when we were at her daughter's house? We were downstairs, asking questions about the daughter's husbands' life insurance policies, when I caught a glimpse of Mrs. Landry, standing at the top of the stairs and smirking."

"Maybe you imagined it," Klein said. "She has no motive, and we have absolutely no evidence pointing in her direction."

"Maybe so, but it was the timing of that smirk," Kristy said. "Before I said the words 'insurance policies,' she seemed tense, wary; I pretended not to notice her but I paid attention. Then, when she heard me ask that particular question, she relaxed, smirked, and immediately disappeared in one of the upstairs bedrooms, but didn't pull the door shut. She listened in on the entire conversation."

"Means, motive, opportunity, Grant," Klein said, sounding like a veritable police academy instructor. "Nowhere have I seen in the manual the word smirk."

"Yeah, but hunch is mentioned a few times, isn't it?" She still didn't want to tell her partner how she'd spent her night, digging into Mrs. Landry's background and looking for anything that could tie her to the murders of her sons-in-law. She'd pored over everything in that woman's life and found absolutely nothing except a parking ticket issued across the street from a dubious club on Hoover Street. But she wasn't going to give up. Maybe the woman was *that* good.

She smiled at Klein tentatively, as if pleading with him. Resigned, he gestured toward the door and Grant grabbed the handle.

"Thanks, partner," she said, before opening the door and entering the small, dreary room.

"Ah, finally," Mrs. Landry said, standing and propping her hands on her hips. "You took your sweet time, didn't you?"

"Thank you for coming in, Mrs. Landry. I appreciate it," Grant said, taking a seat across the table from her guest, who followed suit after a hint of hesitation.

"What is this about?" she asked, feigning a polite smile, while her cold, steel-colored irises threw darts.

"I wanted to give you the opportunity to hear this from us firsthand, not from the tabloids," Kristy said, lowering her voice and drawing closer to Mrs. Landry's head. "We will be arresting your daughter today, I'm afraid."

As she spoke, Kristy held her eyes riveted to the woman's, waiting for a reaction. She knew that whatever that true reaction was, she'd have milliseconds before it disappeared under the mask that the experienced, talented actor would choose to display.

Yet nothing happened when she delivered the blow. No dilated pupils, no eyelash tremor, just cold, intense scrutiny.

"We're charging her with murder," Kristy upped the ante, hoping for a reaction, no matter how small. Again, nothing for a few milliseconds, then the woman pressed a trembling hand upon her chest and tears began rolling down her cheeks.

"No, oh God, no," she sobbed, keeping her eyes squeezed shut as if that gesture could've stopped the flow of tears. "What can I say to convince you my daughter could've never done that? She's a sweet little girl who had a lot of bad luck with men, that's all."

"Mrs. Landry, with all due respect, there's bad luck, and then there's a pattern. Unfortunately, we can't ignore what happened to your daughter's late husbands. All three of them died violent deaths at the hands of street thugs."

"Los Angeles is a horrible place these days," Mrs. Landry said. "Maybe you should be out there, arresting those thugs, instead of blaming my daughter just because she has terrible luck with her choice of husbands," she said in one long breath, riddled with whimpers and flooded with tears.

Kristy watched her closely, forcing her empathy to succumb to reason and be reminded it was one of Hollywood's greatest stage-acting talents who was putting up an Oscar-worthy performance in the interrogation room. Sure, she'd retired a few years ago after a round of plastic surgery delivered less than stellar results, affecting the symmetry of her upper lip. But talent like hers never vanished, it just got better with time, like good wine and aged Kentucky bourbon. Her performance gnawed at Kristy's resolve, sneaking a doubt into her mind and making her wonder if that smirk she thought she'd seen was nothing but her imagination, refusing to believe that one of her favorite Hollywood heroines and the woman's daughter, Paige Landry, was a cold-blooded killer.

As if she'd sensed Kristy's emerging doubt, Mrs. Landry scrutinized her with clinically cold eyes, as she must've checked the impact of her performance on her public while taking a bow, for years in a row.

"It must've been something for Paige," Kristy said, "growing up with someone like you as a mother."

"What do you mean?" Mrs. Landry asked, patting her eyes with a tissue she'd fished out of her Chanel handbag.

"I mean, like, wow," she said, smiling widely. "I can't even imagine what it would be like. Having you as a role model, having you to teach her how to act, how to conquer the hearts and minds of the world in her films."

The smile that had bloomed on the woman's artificially plumped lips died instantly when Kristy mentioned Paige's films.

"That girl," Mrs. Landry said, sounding irritated all of a sudden. "Theater is where real acting takes place, where you perform in front of living, breathing human beings, not in front of... cameras," she spit the word out as if it were bad tasting. "Anyone can act in movies," she added, making a dismissive gesture with her hand, "and everyone does."

"She's incredibly successful though," Kristy said, defending the absent Paige. "I read somewhere she made a few millions last year, didn't she?"

Mrs. Landry frowned for a moment, while one of her perfectly drawn eyebrows arched in disdain.

"Yes, and everyone gawked at her bare breasts, displayed in Dolby Vision for the entire world to see. That's not how I raised her, you know." Her frown lines persisted, and two deep ridges marked the sides of her tense mouth.

"Nevertheless, she owes everything she's done, professionally, to you and no one else," Kristy said, afraid she might push the flattery a bit too far.

The woman's frown quickly disappeared, while a blooming smile stretched her lips, making them appear youthful again. "How right you are, my dear. I gave her acting lessons since she was five, and I introduced her to everyone who was anyone in Hollywood. Her first part? I made that happen for her."

"The role in *Endless Youth*? She was amazing!" Kristy said, watching the woman's reactions closely.

"Pfft," she reacted, making that dismissive gesture with her hand Kristy had seen before. "That wasn't her first role. She played Ophelia for three seasons in a row at the Pantages Theatre. The youngest Ophelia in that theatre's history. These... movies don't count for anything."

Gotcha, Kristy thought, *now I know what makes you tick.* She shifted in her chair and straightened her back, pausing for a moment before proceeding.

"How about the men in Paige's life?" she asked cautiously. "It must've been awesome for her to have your guidance while dating. You seem to know so much!"

"Maybe someone smart like you, my dear, would've listened to her mother. But no, that girl... I told her the day she brought home, um, what was his name, the man who became her first husband?" She looked at Kristy for help, waiting while she opened her notebook and pretended to check her notes.

"You mean Morgan Evans?"

"Yes, him," she said. "A two-bit producer who worshipped the ground under her feet," she said, curling her upper lip and shaking her head in disapproval.

"You didn't like him much, did you?"

"What was there to like?" she replied dryly. "Sure, he had money, but so did she, and so do countless other men in Hollywood. Smarter men, more sophisticated, more intellectual, if you know what I mean. Him? All he talked about was making movies and pushing her to get the roles he wanted for her."

"I remember reading in the papers back then that the media thought they made a great couple. They worked on a few blockbusters together."

"So what? He was still a simpleton, a nobody raking in new money that didn't lend any shine to his hide; quite the opposite."

"But he died," Kristy said, keeping her eyes riveted to hers. "He was killed during a break-in by two assailants who were never caught."

"Yes, that's what happened," Mrs. Landry said. "Great police work; you never caught those two, but now you wish to pin that on my daughter."

"She was traveling at the time; she was filming on location in Australia," Kristy said, although she knew Mrs. Landry had all the details. "Cops call that a little too convenient. It's typical of murders for hire."

"My daughter is innocent," Mrs. Landry said coldly. "Not that she doesn't deserve what's coming to her."

"She does?" Kristy asked, then quickly rephrased. "She does, of course, because she never listened to you, did she?"

"See, my dear, you get it," Mrs. Landry said with a satisfied smile, leaning over and surprising Kristy with a pinch on her cheek.

Kristy laughed and pulled back, uneasy, tempted to charge her with assault.

"How about her second husband, Chad Davenport?"

"Was he the one who got stabbed in the airport restroom?" Mrs. Landry asked, her voice devoid of any emotion. "What a way to go; can you imagine? In a public restroom?"

A hint of a crooked smile fluttered briefly on her lips.

"What?" Kristy asked, smiling encouragingly.

"He deserved that," Mrs. Landry said in a low voice, almost whispering. "He was into drugs, and he made Paige smoke pot a couple of times. Who knows where she'd be today, if he were still alive. In some trailer park, maybe? Teeth gone, hair unkempt, wearing those horrible T-shirts without a brassiere?"

"You're probably right," Kristy said, "and you're also probably the only one who saw who he really was. Only a devoted mother would think like that," she said, careful not to show her real emotions. The man had been a successful publicist, working for one of LA's largest advertising agencies. He probably didn't deserve any of Mrs. Landry's contempt.

"How right you are, dearie," Mrs. Landry replied, sending a full-blown smile her way. "But he wasn't nearly as bad as this Justin Keller, the musician, my daughter's latest acquisition. That girl, she just won't listen to me, no matter what. I told her, time and again, to stop dating these no-good losers."

"Too bad she didn't listen," Kristy said. "Was he being difficult with your daughter?"

"Not with her, I don't think. Just incredibly disrespectful with me," she replied. "He had concerts, he went on tour everywhere, trying to promote his so-called music, and wanted her to go with him, to ignore her own career, to… abandon me."

Her voice broke, and for a split second, Kristy was able to see underneath Mrs. Landry's mask.

"Oh, no, she would've never done that," Kristy encouraged her, "not after everything you've done for her."

"But she did. She went with him to the UK for his concerts, then went again when he won some British music award. He's an Englishman, you know."

"He was, yes. And he got mugged and killed in the street, right here in LA, after he came back from tour. How do you think that happened, Mrs. Landry?"

Mrs. Landry pulled back, leaning against the backrest of her chair and folded her arms at her chest. "You're ready to arrest my daughter for his murder and you don't know?"

"We know one of his assailants is a former high-school colleague of your daughter," Kristy replied. "We put two and two together. Your daughter has access to large amounts of cash, and she could've arranged everything so easily."

"And the life insurance policy—" Mrs. Landry started to say.

"Was for five million dollars," Kristy continued the phrase, "a decent payday, even for an actor who hasn't landed a single role this past year."

"Then there's nothing I could say to convince you that my daughter's innocent, is there?" Mrs. Landry said, raising her arms in the air a bit overly dramatic, then letting them drop back on the table, as if under the weight of evidence.

Kristy looked at her for a moment, pacing herself and thinking through her moves.

"You know what I see? I see brilliance in whoever orchestrated these deaths. I see amazing intelligence in the way those losers were eliminated from the face of the earth, and as far as I'm concerned, whoever did this did the world a favor." As she spoke, Mrs. Landry's smile widened, as if she were getting ready to take a bow after the curtain drop. "I just wish I knew more about this amazing plan, that's all. The perfect murders, right? Cops talk about them all the time, but I've never seen perfect murders until now."

"I don't understand, my dear. What do you need?"

"We have no evidence, nothing. We couldn't arrest anyone for the murders of Morgan Evans and Chad Davenport, no matter what happens, because we have nothing. But you're an amazing woman, Mrs. Landry. Would you mind if we speculated a little about how it might have happened? Only someone as brilliant as you could help someone like me understand."

She smiled and nodded, showing two rows of veneered teeth, or probably implants, judging by how perfect they were.

"Three men, all doing well financially, all signed hefty insurance policies naming your daughter as the beneficiary. One is shot during a break-in, another stabbed to death in an airport restroom, and the third killed in a street mugging gone wrong. The break-in was on video, captured by the home's surveillance system. We never caught the perps, but we saw they were two African American males, average height and weight."

"I knew that," Mrs. Landry said, sounding almost impatient although she still smiled.

"Then we have one white assailant going into the airport restroom with Chad Davenport, also on video surveillance from the airport cameras. Finally, members of the Satanas Gang, three Filipino men, attacked and killed Justin Keller." She paused a little, for effect. "Mrs. Landry, I don't believe your daughter killed her husbands, but I'm the only one here who believes in her innocence."

"Tell me, how can I help?" Mrs. Landry said, leaning forward, imploring with her outstretched hands, her manicured nails flawless in the dim light.

"If I could come up with a scenario that would explain how this was possible, then we can exculpate your daughter, enough to create some reasonable doubt. This won't even go to trial, I promise."

Mrs. Landry grabbed Kristy's hand and squeezed it gently. "You're amazing, my dear, thank you."

"Oh, no, Mrs. Landry, you are," she said, feigning modesty the best that she could. "So, tell me, how would you send a couple of gangsters after someone, without paying them off? Without leaving any money trail, any phone records?"

"With people, you give them what they want. Or, at least you *promise* them what they want," she said, sounding a little arrogant. "Everyone wants money in this godforsaken city, my dear. You don't absolutely have to give them *your* money, right? Just... make promises. Anyone can do that, you know."

Kristy cupped her mouth in her hand, stunned. The killer was right there, in front of her eyes, but now she needed proof. She took her notebook out and scribbled something quickly on a piece of paper, then held it against the one-way mirror until she heard Klein's double tap against the glass. A minute later, he entered the interrogation room and handed Kristy a piece of paper that had a single word written on it: "Yes." Quietly, he left the room, smiling to himself on the way out.

"It would take a brilliant actor," Kristy said, while folding the paper and tucking it inside her pocket, "a stage actor no less, to sell something like that, wouldn't it?"

Mrs. Landry smiled and nodded a bit sideways, fluttering her eyelids as if accepting a huge compliment.

"It takes guts to show up by oneself in the middle of a club, surrounded by gangbangers, and start selling one's game. Playing one's part impeccably, in front of an audience that could rip you to shreds at the tiniest mistake."

A glint of pride colored Mrs. Landry's irises.

"It would have to be simple, a simple message that they could easily understand," Kristy continued. "Concern for a loved one who's traveling with millions in cash," she continued, then saw a flicker of agreement in her eyes. She was on the right track. "Ask their advice, which would flatter them and make them wonder if you're sane, then drink with them and let the name slip out. Ask their help too, maybe?"

Mrs. Landry looked away briefly.

"No, you didn't have to go that far, just a carefully timed slip of the tongue and the promise of millions in cash, and they were hooked. They believed you, Mrs. Landry, didn't they? Because they knew you, they knew who you were. They bought your story." She stood, pacing the room excitedly. "And there it was, the perfect murder for hire, without a paper trail, without money changing hands. Brilliant!"

To her amazement, Mrs. Landry stood and took a tiny bow. "You see how my daughter couldn't have done any of this, right? But you can't prove I did either. Anyone could do what you said."

Kristy breathed, satisfied with having closed the case and wondering what Klein was thinking, on the other side of the mirror.

"We caught one of the Filipinos who killed Justin Keller, and he didn't confess to anything. But my partner just asked him where his gang hangs out, and that much he shared. It's a bar and lounge on Hoover Street. Too bad you got a ticket there for illegal parking, a week before Justin was killed."

She watched Mrs. Landry's blood drain from her face.

"I'm willing to bet the bartender will remember your performance. I've seen you act live, Mrs. Landry, and you're unforgettable."

NUMBER FIVE

J en stared at the six men through the one-way mirror, ignoring the panic ravaging her mind. None of them could see her; she knew the drill. She studied their faces with raw curiosity mixed with dread, while her trembling hand caressed her daughter's head with rhythmic, calming strokes. Kayla was wrapped around her leg, holding on tight, the way she'd been doing since that dreadful Wednesday night.

She couldn't believe that was only two days ago.

The lineup presented six almost identical men, at least at first glance; white males in their mid-forties, with unkempt, brown hair and brown eyes. Beards covered their faces with a variety of facial hair: a goatee on number two; a short stubble on the first man in line; a full beard on two other men; even a split, French beard on number six. Where did the cops find these men when they needed to bring in a witness for an ID?

Her daughter's right hand let go of her pants leg and pointed at the window. She felt a lump in her throat; her daughter had recognized the man too. If she'd known that, she would've left Kayla outside in the waiting room, in the care of a police officer. The last thing she wanted was to retraumatize her little girl.

She folded Kayla's extended finger and held on to her tiny hand while shielding her eyes from the view. She didn't need her baby's help to recognize the man; she'd known him from the first second he'd stepped into the room and took his position in front of the white wall lined with black, horizontal markers meant to assist witnesses in approximating suspects' heights.

"Do you recognize anyone?" The district attorney spoke in a soft, encouraging voice. "Please, take your time." She quickly glanced at the man, then looked at the detective assigned to the case. Farther back, behind the officer, two other men stood waiting, their gazes not nearly as friendly and supportive, and their expensive suits telling a different story than the cop's worn-out slacks and pilling shirt. They must've been the suspect's lawyers, attending the lineup to ensure no foul play took place, no influencing of the witness by the police.

She turned and looked at the men behind the window again, thinking hard, fear screaming inside her skull, urging her to do the logical thing that she could do as a mother, a wife, a survivor: picking the wrong man out of the lineup, permanently compromising herself as a witness. Saving her life, protecting her family.

That's what Tom would want; hell, that's what he'd do in her shoes, without a moment's hesitation. He'd say, "Screw everyone, let them all go to hell. Let us be safe; that's all that matters."

She shivered, missing him more than she wanted to admit. He was in Arizona somewhere, driving a truck, hauling frozen food in his eighteen-wheel reefer. She could've called him, could've told him what had happened, but then what would he have done? Driven home like a maniac, faking the logs and putting his life and other drivers at risk, just to get home to her an hour sooner? She couldn't take that chance with Tom's life; like most trucker wives, highway accidents and mangled, burning wreckage populated her nightmares. The risks he took to keep them fed and clothed were high enough without her contributions.

She squeezed her eyes shut, remembering how it all started. It didn't take much effort to do so; every time her eyelids lowered, the image of that man came to her mind, fresh, in vivid color and sharp detail, as if she'd witnessed the entire scene through a magnifying glass, and time had slowed its passing to ensure she absorbed every word that was said and even the tiniest facts.

It happened on Wednesday, at about six in the afternoon.

She worked retail at a small, local apparel store, and her days off were midweek, when they existed at all. Her boss, one of the most insecure people who'd ever walked the earth, had absolutely no respect for his employee's personal time; he expected her to reply to his emails and text messages every day, around the clock, as if she were a doctor or a firefighter, or someone really important.

That was her only excuse for staring at her phone while she'd taken Kayla for a walk in Cherokee Park, Louisville's most prized landmark after Churchill Downs. Cherokee was huge, more than four hundred acres and a pleasure to walk through, its pathways and meadows designed to perfection by none other than Frederick Law Olmsted, the father of landscape architecture. She knew it well; she'd grown up screaming like a banshee while running up and down the gentle slopes, climbing the trees, and hiding in the bushes.

She'd followed Beargrass Creek with Kayla that day, strolling on the paved walkway, typing furiously on her phone, sending reply after reply to her insufferable boss. Every few moments, she raised her eyes from the screen and looked at Kayla; her daughter was having a blast, squealing in the late afternoon sun, pounding on a rubber ball, its bounces sending a cadence of echoing beats against the distant hills. Entirely focused on her phone, she kept her ear to her daughter's trail of sounds, walking slowly, utterly oblivious to her surroundings.

Then she heard something else, a muffled whimper coming from somewhere very close. Something in that sound sent a chill through her veins. She stopped and looked around carefully. Kayla was playing a few yards behind her. No one else walked the path at that time, but she sensed a presence; someone was nearby.

She let her phone slide into her jacket pocket and stepped on the grass, heading toward the neatly trimmed bushes scattered on the meadow a few yards away. As she turned to go around a few massive oak trees, she heard the whimper again, a little louder this time. One more step to the side, and her eyes locked on a woman's feet, her underwear wrapped around her ankles, thrashing and kicking as she struggled to free herself. Another step closer, and she could see the assailant, straddling her, holding her hands above her head in a tight grip and covering her mouth so she couldn't scream.

Jen looked back toward Kayla and saw she was at least fifteen yards away. She knew she should've walked away while the man hadn't yet seen her, grabbed Kayla, and called the cops. But that meant leaving that poor woman there, in the hands of the monster who was viciously attacking her.

Instead, Jen took another step closer. "Hey," she shouted, pulling out her phone. "Get the hell away from her. I'm calling the cops."

The man turned and looked at her with deathly eyes, filled with a frenzy of mixed emotions. By all appearances, he would've gladly killed her where she stood. For a brief moment, she wondered if the man had a gun. She'd been stupid, reckless, approaching the man and lashing out. She'd always known her big mouth was going to get her in trouble one day, and that day might've just arrived.

He looked at his victim again, still covering her mouth with his hand, then back at Jen. Then he stood up quickly and lunged at Jen with his fists clenched, bellowing. She screamed, a bloodcurdling scream that sent echoes throughout the park. The girl lying on the ground screamed too.

Then he hit Jen, one single punch to her temple that had her unconscious before she hit the ground.

When she came to, she couldn't get up; it was as if her entire body had been stomped into a mass of dull pain. In the distance, Kayla still played with her ball, oblivious to what was happening. Jen tried to lift her head, worried that the man might still be there, but she couldn't; jolts of pain sent lightning flashes through her eyes whenever she tried to move.

She saw her phone, facedown in the grass a couple of feet away, out of reach. Keeping her eyes on Kayla, she whispered, "Hey, Siri, call nine-one-one." She listened for the familiar chime that didn't come. She repeated the command, this time louder, and eventually, the device confirmed the call. Then she faded out before she could say another word.

She woke up in the hospital, Kayla sleeping on a small couch next to her bed. Her head throbbed, and her mouth was dry, but she was alive, ready to go home. Getting out of bed proved a difficult task, but she forged ahead; Kayla had her nightly routine, and Jen needed a shower and a stiff drink, neither of which were offered to an inpatient in the trauma center.

She recalled being rolled out of the hospital in a wheelchair, holding Kayla's small hand, while a nurse kept insisting that she should spend the night. In hindsight, she couldn't understand why she didn't accept the invitation, especially after the nurse made a stop to show Jen the woman she'd saved.

She was nineteen years old, and her name was Sabrina Cassese, the only daughter of an Italian family.

She was unconscious, sunk in a coma after receiving a kick to the head that had resulted in a subdural hematoma. The help Jen had called for had arrived, but there was a chance it had been too late.

Jen looked at the girl's pale face and felt a wave of anger building inside her, burning her eyes with the threat of tears. Then she gestured at the nurse, and soon she breathed the fresh autumn air while waiting for a cab.

Her car was still at Cherokee Park. She'd have to get it in the morning.

Then she realized her purse was gone.

The obliging nurse checked and confirmed with the first

responders that no purse had been found at the scene, while Jen struggled to breathe, sheer terror choking her. That bastard knew where she lived. He had her address, her wallet, her house keys. With a look of concern on her face, the nurse called the cops.

A few hours later, she put Kayla to bed after an emergency-service locksmith had replaced her locks, and the cops had committed to drive by her place at least once an hour.

It was daylight already.

The sun shone brightly, dissipating any remnants of darkness and fear, sending reassuring messages that everything was going to be okay. She'd thought of calling Tom that Thursday morning, to tell him what had happened, but she didn't want him stressed out while driving. Instead, she brewed herself a pot of stiff coffee and, wrapped in a warm blanket, resigned herself to watching Kayla play in the backyard. When he called her later that day, she managed to lie herself through the call and hung up missing him more than before.

One by one, her memories invaded, unwanted stragglers she didn't want anywhere near her heart. The face of that man, the color of his hair, his eyes, his beard. The smell of him, a tangy, sweaty smell of grime and metabolized alcohol. His voice as he cursed her.

Then other memories, just as painful. One of the medics saying that they'd found Kayla curled up against her body, lying in the grass, sucking her thumb. Another one saying she'd saved that poor woman's life. A gray-haired, potbellied detective taking her statement. A young doctor telling her she had to wear a cervical collar for a few weeks, because of the whiplash she'd suffered when that man had punched her. Finally, a forensic technician who'd collected a swab of blood from her temple with a satisfied grin, because the blood wasn't Jen's; he believed it could've been her attacker's.

Thursday's daylight had come and gone, and the darkness scared her. The cops had been by a few times, even stopped to say hi and ask her if she needed anything. She had their numbers loaded in her phone, ready to call, but she didn't think she'd need them. Then the detective who'd taken her statement called and invited her to identify her attacker from a lineup at the precinct on Friday morning.

She'd replied, "Yeah, sure, okay."

Without thinking what that meant.

Petrified, she sat on the couch, wrapping her arms around Kayla's little body, rocking her back and forth until she fell asleep in her arms. She didn't dare to move anymore, afraid she'd wake Kayla to a reality she wasn't ready to face herself.

Minutes flew by in a daze; it was almost midnight when she realized her windows had remained uncovered, and anyone who drove down the street could see in to her home. Gently, she eased Kayla's body off her knees onto the couch and put a pillow under her head. Then, shivering and clenching her jaws to keep her teeth from chattering, she rushed to close the curtains. She started in the living room and worked her way quickly around the house, leaving the bedrooms for last.

When she returned to the living room, thinking she should take Kayla to bed, she froze.

The back door was ajar, the wind blowing in a few scattered leaves, littering the white granite tiles. She'd changed the lock, but the frail door only needed a shoulder shove to bust open, even with the deadbolt on.

That man was there, sitting by her daughter on the couch, holding a gun to her head.

She gasped, covering her mouth with her hand and faltering.

"Hello, Mrs. Tilley," he said with a lewd grin. "It's Mrs., right?"

She nodded, her throat dry, her breath caught. "Uh-huh."

She swallowed hard. "What do you want?"

"You know what I want," he replied calmly, keeping his voice low, not to wake Kayla. "I want you to forget you ever saw me. That simple. No need to scare the little one." He stood and walked toward her, pointing his gun at her chest. Then he grazed against her breast with the barrel and licked his lips. "Think you could do that for me, Mrs. Tilley?"

She nodded again, so vigorously that her hair came loose from the pin holding it in a bun. "Y—yes, I can." She cleared her constricted throat, darting a worried look at Kayla. "I won't say a thing, I swear."

He scoffed, his disbelief obvious. "Because if you do," he continued, running the muzzle of the gun against her skin, her face, then back on her chest where the bathrobe had become undone, leaving the see-through lace of her nightgown exposed, "you won't make it to trial, to testify. Accidents can happen." He grabbed a handful of her hair and twisted, turning his fist until it hurt, and she whimpered. "Catch my drift?"

"Y—yes," she sobbed, forced to turn her head as he kept pulling her hair, sending pulses of pain through her bruised neck.

He yanked her down abruptly, and she fell to her knees, unable to free herself from his grip. He brought his face close to hers and grinned evilly, showing crooked teeth and emitting waves of alcohol breath. She reached behind her head with both her hands, trying to loosen his grip but failed, her efforts eliciting cackles and snorts, nothing more.

Then he shoved her head to the floor and stared down at her, his face a frozen warning affirmed by deadly, menacing eyes. "You better fucking remember that tomorrow," he hissed. "And don't go calling no cops tonight, you hear me? I'll be watching."

Trembling, she watched him leave through the back door and close it behind him. Her knees weak, she stayed on the floor for a moment, staring at the door with eyes rounded in fear, her sobs stifled by the hand she pressed tightly over her mouth.

Their lives would never be the same again.

"Why are you crying, Mommy?" she heard Kayla ask. Her little girl stood by her for a brief moment, then she wrapped her arms around her mother's neck.

Jen got up, and they returned to the couch. She rocked her daughter back and forth, unable to think of anything to say, gently caressing her silky hair, soothing her, feeling her agitated breaths returning to normal.

Jen did that now, staring at those six men through the one-way mirror, her daughter's angst renewed.

"Do any of these men look familiar?" the DA repeated his earlier question, probably because she was taking so long to answer.

She knew what she had to do. Point at a complete stranger and discredit herself. There would be no trial, no one to testify against, no need to fear that man again. If she refused to point him out, he'd have no reason to kill her. Her silence was her life insurance, hers and her family's.

But a rapist and a killer would go free. She had no doubt that man had taken lives; something in her gut had recognized the lust for blood in the man's eyes the night before; his threats were real, his hand firm on the gun handle, his voice eager with the anticipation of spilled blood.

She closed her eyes for a moment, hoping she'd conjure Tom's loving face and his sound advice in her weary mind. Instead, she saw Sabrina's body, lying in a hospital bed, hooked up to machines that did her breathing for her.

"Please forgive me, baby," she whispered, wiping a tear from her eyes, begging Tom's forgiveness as if he were there by her side. Soon he would be, questioning her judgment, doubting her sanity.

"Could you repeat that?" the DA asked. "We didn't hear

you."

She took a deep breath, reassessing the decision she'd reached, the only one she'd be able to live with, even if that meant her life would be uprooted from Kentucky and moved to Arizona, at the other end of Tom's long-haul route.

Out of the six men she was staring at, one wanted her to be a coward, to sell out everything she believed in. That bastard didn't deserve to go free; he deserved to pay for everything he'd done.

When she spoke, her voice was clear, strong, showing nothing of her internal turmoil.

"It's number five."

MY GIRLS

I killed a man today.

My breath still catches when I think of it, but I can think of nothing else. The bloodstain slowly spreading around his torso, engulfing increasingly more of the oriental pattern on our living room rug. The metallic smell that clung to my nostrils and just won't go away, despite the effluvium of stale odors emanating from the back seat of the police cruiser, where I sit handcuffed, awaiting my fate.

It stinks of vomit in here, of sweat embedded deeply into the seat's upholstery, of fear pheromones, of human despair. Still, I consider myself lucky somehow, because it's a torrid day, well into the nineties. The cops left the engine running and the AC on before shoving me in here and slamming the door shut.

That was more than an hour ago, or so I believe. Funny how one can lose track of time after taking a man's life.

I worm my way to the center of the back seat, where the flow of ice-cold air is stronger, and close my eyes, resigned to be haunted yet again by the ghost of the man I have killed.

I don't see that terrifying bloodstain against the backdrop of my tightly shut eyelids; no, I see Diana making coffee for us in the dim morning light, wearing a silk nightie, the one I bought for her from Victoria's Secret on our fifteenth wedding anniversary, an extravagance we don't usually afford. I remember how the day had started, how it had shown all signs of being an ordinary Tuesday, maybe the stuff of boredom, of routine-ridden, middle-class family life, not the stuff of the nightmare it was going to become.

She always brewed us a fresh pot at six. She was the morning person, while I, the notorious night owl, abused the snooze button, stubbornly holding on to the sheets and dreading the moment I'd have to slip into the shower and let water rinse the last remnant of slumber away. But the smell of that fresh coffee was my tradeoff; I loved starting my days with Diana watching me with scrutinizing eyes from across the table, and mumbling funny, empty threats like, "You'd better get that shopping list done, mister, or else."

I grinned like I always did, challenging her for the heck of it. "Or else what?"

Her phone chimed. She frowned, glancing up at the wall clock in the shape of a cat's face, its black whiskers pointing out the hours and minutes. That model of kitsch consumerism only showed 6:17, way too early for anyone to be sending her text messages.

She read the message while I waited impatiently, summoning all my willpower to not reach out and snatch the phone out of her hand, driven by an urge to yell at the unknown sender for disturbing our morning routine.

Then she stopped breathing, or so I thought. Blood drained from her face, leaving her skin pale, cadaveric, as if touched by death itself.

I swallowed with difficulty, feeling my throat inexplicably dry.

"What's going on, Di?" I asked in a grating whisper.

She bit her lip and looked left, then right, more like a cornered animal trying to escape than my usually calm wife. The terror in her eyes was unmistakable, and when she spoke, her voice shattered, her words broken by raspy breaths of air. "Promise me you'll hear me out before saying anything, okay?"

I stood, forcefully pushing the chair away from the table. It made a long, screeching sound against the kitchen floor's ceramic tiles. I walked around the table and stopped right in front of her, extending my hand like a parent would to a child, demanding her phone.

Not my proudest moment, I know, but patience has never

been my virtue. If some asshole was causing my wife such terror, I needed to know his number, if you get my drift.

She shook her head slowly, staring at the mosaic floor, and shoved the phone in her pocket, her fingers wrapped tightly around it. "Hear me out, first. Please. It's not easy for me."

Her fear contaminated my soul, grabbing my chest in a merciless grip. What was going on? All I could do was nod, as I pulled a chair closer to her and sat. I reached across the table corner and grabbed her hand, as cold as ice. "I'm right here, Di; just tell me what's wrong."

A long moment passed in perfect, torturous stillness.

"A few days ago," she finally whispered, still staring at the floor while gently pulling her hand out of mine, "I met someone."

Three words, that's all it took to feel like I'd been kicked in the nuts. I drew a deep breath of air as soon as I was able to, getting ready to bellow the only question that bounced around in my brain. Why?

"Please," she said, before I had the chance to say anything. "Please, let me tell you." She put her frozen fingers on my forearm, and, for a split second, that familiar touch seemed foreign, unwanted. "Nothing happened," she said quickly, looking at me with worried eyes. "And nothing ever will. It wasn't like that."

I finally let go of that breath of air I'd been holding in my lungs, and it came out sounding like a pained sigh. I didn't believe her. I couldn't. Not anymore.

"He asked me out for coffee, on my lunch break, and I said yes."

"You work together?" I asked dryly.

"Not really. He was there to pick up something for a client of ours, and we got to talking."

"So, first time you lay eyes on this guy and you go out with him? Jeez, Diana…"

She lowered her head while tears started rolling down her cheeks.

"Why?" I finally asked, surprised that the simple act of saying that one word could be so demanding, so painful.

When she eventually looked at me, I almost didn't recognize her. It was as if her beautiful visage had been recomposed into a stranger's face, using the same familiar features, but somehow yielding a different result.

"You don't know how it's been for me, all these years. With Isabel…"

"Don't you dare blame any of this on our daughter, you hear me?"

She turned her face away from me and didn't say another word, although it was obvious that I waited for her explanation.

"Okay, what's with Isabel?" I finally gave in and asked.

"Nothing, you're right, it's not her fault. But I stopped living," she said, wiping her tears with the back of her hand in a quick gesture to regain her composure. "I stopped feeling alive. At first it was diapers, then formula, then teething, then potty training, then school and homework and play dates, and it went on and on, and I… just didn't feel alive anymore. I just wanted to feel wanted, I guess. Be a woman again."

My jaw slacked. How did I not see this?

Or did I?

Was I being honest with myself, with Diana? Maybe I did see it but didn't bother to acknowledge it because that would've meant having to do something about it. She was always so calm about things, always smiling, encouraging me, making Isabel feel special, being the glue that held our family together. Finding out it was all a façade was a shock, albeit an understandable shock.

But then again, she was good at lying, apparently. "Tell me about this guy. Who is he?"

"He's no one you know, and I didn't think it would matter," she said, sniffling quietly. "We had coffee, and that was it. We had a nice visit and then went our separate ways, or so I thought."

I frowned and shot her an inquisitive look. "What do you mean?"

"Before leaving the café, he acted a little strange, and I got a creepy feeling," she said, shooting me a quick, embarrassed glance before staring at the floor again. "We stood to leave, and he came in front of me, touched my face, and then started to remove my jacket, touching me in an intimate sort of way. Then he just laughed it off."

"What?" I snapped. "Right there, in the middle of... where the hell were you, anyway?"

"Starbucks, the one near my office. You know the place." She filled her lungs with air before continuing. "I pulled away, walked off, and never looked back. I later realized that I'd lost my wallet but didn't go back to look for it until the following morning. I never did find it."

The silence fell heavy again, and I knew there was more. I drilled her with my eyes in an unspoken question.

"He's blackmailing me," she said, finally giving me that damn phone of hers, the extortion photo emanating from the flat screen. "He must've had someone take pictures of us. He wants five grand, or he'll tell you we're having an affair."

I stared at the photo, feeling my hands go numb. My wife, looking at another man with an expression on her face I'd thought, in my immense arrogance, was reserved only for me. His right hand, barely touching her cheek. His left hand, gently driving her jacket off her shoulder, exposing the bare skin of her arm. In the background, the walls appear to be a hotel room, not the local Starbucks.

I squinted, but the photo was too small for me to tell with any accuracy if it had been Photoshopped against a different background. I stared at Diana for a long moment, at a loss for words.

"I swear to you, Dylan, that's all there is to tell. I'm really sorry," she added, and the floodgates opened. Her shoulders heaved with uncontrollable sobs, while I sat there watching, trying to decide whom to trust.

Fifteen years should be worth something, I thought, deciding to trust her after all.

I squeezed her hand and she raised her eyes to look at me. I only saw shame in her blue irises, embarrassment, and guilt. No lies. The truth was bad enough.

"You've obviously been set up," I said, then started texting in response to his threat to inform me, the husband, about the so-called affair. "I bet he's the one who lifted your wallet."

Don't care if you tell him, I texted the reply, *I have no money for you.*

Then I willed myself to open my arms and hold Diana close to my chest, feeling her tears soak my shirt as her sobs continued for a few minutes. I closed my eyes and caressed her hair absentmindedly, forcing myself to think this was an ugly episode soon to be forgotten, soon to be buried under the label, "Shit that happens in people's lives," right along with unprovoked road rage incidents, power outages, and office backstabbing.

When she pulled away from me, she gasped loudly and took two rushed steps backward, not stopping until she backed into the kitchen counter. I turned to see what she was staring at and froze.

The man in the photo was sitting at my damn kitchen table, smiling, showing a perfect set of white teeth, and resting his hand on the handle of a 6-inch tactical knife.

"I heard you're okay with threesomes," he said calmly, his steeled glance meeting mine without any hesitation.

"Get the hell out of this house," I said, clenching my fists without even realizing it.

He rapped his fingernails against the shiny blade and interrupted me. "I don't think you're in a position to set terms, Mr. White," he replied. "And, by the way, you need a new lock on that side door."

I still had Diana's phone in my hand. "I'll call the cops—"

"You won't do anything," he said. With a quick, martial arts move, he hit me across my forearm so hard I dropped the phone. I heard Diana whimpering behind me, and I took one step toward the man, trying to shield her from him.

"What do you want?" I asked quietly. I read somewhere that if you can manage to lower your voice in a tense situation, the opponent instinctively believes you're stronger than you really are. Goes back to our animal instincts. Larger predators have lower-pitched voices, and our DNA still remembers the danger of encountering a predator with a large chest cavity.

Unfortunately, he didn't seem too impressed with my imitation of a hefty predator. He held his knife up to his eyes, looking closely at how the light reflected against its blade, and then ran his thumb against the blade, as if to see if it was sharp enough. His pupils were dilated, undoubtedly under the effect of some drug, not a great indicator of logical thought processes.

"Money," he eventually said.

"Okay," I said, maybe a little too quickly. I just wanted him gone, out of our lives for good. Before seven thirty, if possible, before Isabel came downstairs for breakfast.

My heart stopped at the thought of Isabel and Diana being in the same room with that man. *Please, God, no.*

"Five grand ain't going to cut it no more," he said coldly, "since I had to come all the way here and everything. Say, fifty grand?"

That was our entire savings account. I swallowed and uttered angrily, "Okay, fifty grand. I need to go to the bank to pull that out." I conveniently left out the fact that the bank would be closed for another couple of hours; that particular detail was not something he'd want to hear.

"Sure, go ahead," he gestured, pointing the blade toward the door. "I'll stay here with Diana. She'll keep me entertained."

As he said her name, his lips curled in a lascivious grin that made my stomach turn. How could Diana even have coffee with someone like that?

I studied him for a moment. I had to admit he was attractive, in a bad boy kind of way. I knew from watching countless chick flicks with my girls that his type held some appeal with middle-aged women, and young ones too. Thick, muscular arms attached to his wide chest, he was by far stronger than me, an almost scrawny actuarial data analyst, who worked in a dusty room without windows, calculating the risk of average individuals to expire at any given time. But I knew how to calculate risk and do it fast, not to mention I have in me a good game of poker for the same essential reasons.

My most immediate risk was Isabel. He couldn't set his filthy eyes on her or, God forbid, his lewd hands should touch her. I had to put some distance between him and my wife, for the same reasons. In conclusion, I had to get him out of the house, pronto.

"No can do," I said. "You come with me to the bank if you want that money."

I did my best to convey a thousand words in a quick glance I threw Diana over my shoulder, then I turned back toward him and shrugged. "If I leave here by myself, I might not come back," I added, and spat on the floor to the side, something I never, ever do. "After all, she cheated on me, so... you understand how I feel." I pressed my lips together and clenched my jaws, expressing as much contempt as I could muster, and that wasn't difficult at all, looking at him.

He was thrown off by my unexpected response, and, by the look of it, he hadn't really thought his strategy through. Silence was thick and palpable; you could hear a pin drop.

Unfortunately, something else was heard, distant, barely intelligible yet recognizable in the perfect stillness of the room.

"Nine-one-one; what's your emergency?"

Fast as lightning, the man lunged past me, shoving me out of his way and grabbing Diana by the neck, unintentionally leaving the knife on the table. I stared at that blade as if hypnotized.

"Where is it? Where's the damn phone?" he shouted, an inch from Diana's pale face.

I had left my phone by the coffee maker, and she'd somehow managed to dial 911, hiding behind me while I was talking with the stranger. Paralyzed, I didn't dare reach for the knife, afraid he'd be quicker than me and break her neck like a twig before I could finish him off.

She babbled something and eventually pointed toward the phone, tucked behind the appliance.

The man took it, threw it to the floor, and crushed it under his boot, without letting go of her throat. I could hear her choking, gasping for air. I was running out of time.

Afraid he'd see me go for the knife and absent any better options, I jumped at him from behind, grabbing his throat with both my hands, squeezing as tightly as I could, while letting my entire weight hang against his body, hoping he'd let go of Diana's neck.

He did, for a brief moment; long enough for him to shake me off easier than a dog shakes off water after a summer dip. He slammed me against the wall and I fell to the ground, dizzy, seeing stars. Then he reached for Diana again. She screamed and hit him with the dirty skillet I'd left in the sink the night before. Unfazed, he wobbled toward the table, grabbed his knife, and pressed the blade against Diana's neck, demanding that she dropped the skillet.

From the top of the stairs, I heard a high-pitched voice.

"Mom? Daddy?"

Oh, no.

"Run, baby, run," I shouted, before the man kicked me in the stomach. I heard a rib crack and for a moment, I didn't feel the pain. That came later—intense, sharp, and almost blinding me with every shallow, panting breath.

"You're going to give me everything you have in this house, you hear me? Cash, jewelry, credit cards, everything."

I looked and saw my twelve-year-old daughter, whimpering, her hands trembling badly as she tried to unlock the front door's dead bolt. For some reason, she'd walked right past the open side entrance and crossed the living room to use the front door. The moment I saw her, he saw her too.

He let go of Diana's throat and licked his lips. "What do we have here, huh?" he said, walking toward Isabel, twisting the knife in his hand and grinning in anticipation. "Umm... just like I want 'em," he added, grabbing Isabel's arm and throwing her on the couch. "You're going to like this," he mumbled, unzipping his pants.

That moment I didn't care about anything; all I could hear was Isabel's screams and her mother's desperate, pleading sobs. I didn't care that I was half his size, or that he'd likely stab me to death before I gave him as much as a shiner. I didn't care about his blade, or the expert way he wielded it. I only cared about my girls.

Through some twist of favorable fate, he hadn't tied us up, and that was the only advantage we had. He must've assumed the cracked rib had immobilized me and that Diana was too hysterical to do anything to stop him from hurting our baby girl. He was wrong.

I looked around and saw our kitchen not as a place of quiet family dinners but as a weapons depot, ripe with choices. The heavy, cast iron Dutch oven that Diana had inherited from her mother could probably crack a skull as thick as his. I shot Diana a glance, then grabbed the cauldron from the stovetop, while she picked up the skillet and followed me, brave, unwavering, just as that brute pinned my daughter's arms against the couch. I didn't hesitate; I let the pot fall down heavy, with all my might, then raised it and let it fall again.

The knife rattled as he dropped it on the hardwood floor. He fell and rolled on his side at my feet, then started to squirm, reaching for my ankle and gripping it with an iron fist. I picked up his knife and stabbed him in the chest, not once, but three or four times, until he moved no more.

Then everything is a blur; the cops finally came in response to the suspiciously disconnected 911 call. Initially, they said it was self-defense and we were fine, but then someone found Diana's phone on the floor. They saw that damn photo and handcuffed me immediately, saying that I had lured my wife's lover-turned-blackmailer to kill him and that was premeditation. They mentioned something about murder when they read my Miranda rights. I was too tired to care, in too much pain after the adrenaline had worn off.

Then... this. The back seat of a police cruiser, thankfully with the air conditioning on, while my wife and daughter were probably being hauled to the emergency room. As for me, I didn't think to ask the cops for medical assistance, although my ribs feel like they're piercing my insides, and my face is burning and throbbing where he crushed me against the wall.

A cop opened the cruiser door and beckoned me out. I squinted into the bright sunlight and managed to extricate myself, welcoming the humid heat of the Philadelphia summer. He removed my handcuffs, and I rubbed my wrists vigorously to make the numbness go away.

"You're free to go, sir," he said. "Shane Clay was wanted for murder in New York State and has two active warrants here. We'll need you at the precinct to give a formal statement. Is Friday okay with you?"

"Sure," I mumbled, looking around for the ambulance.

There it is, parked behind the Crime Scene van. I rush toward it, limping and struggling to breathe in the hot, thick air, but then I see them. I open my arms to welcome them both as they run toward me.

My girls.

My daughter, who mixes up the simplest of requests, even in a dire situation. What part of "run, baby, run" was confusing? She could've gone out the open side door, the door she always uses, but she went through the living room. She can be obstinate, but I suspect she was being a daredevil by going all the way to the front door, to lure Shane away from her mom and me.

My wife of fifteen years, who's been the light of my life since she said, "I do," but chose to not tell me how trapped she felt in our chock-full-of-chores life, wanting to "be a woman again," instead went out for coffee with a man who turned out to be a murderer named Shane Clay.

Both stubborn, gutsy, hotheaded, daring, self-reliant, fearless, defiant... and the list of adjectives can go on and on. But not a single moment of my life would be worth anything without my girls.

AWAKE

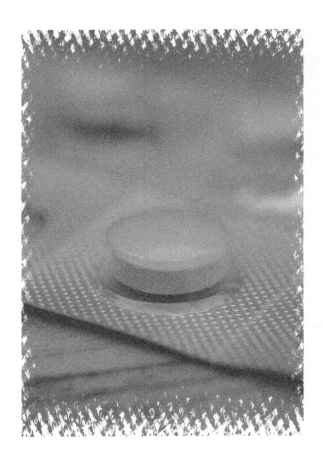

T he first thing she noticed was the missing knife. The Santoku knife, the biggest blade of the set she'd recently purchased amid her husband's protests. But he wasn't the one chopping veggies and slicing meat all day long to feed four hungry mouths. She'd told him that much, and he'd given her the silent treatment for a while, at least until she completed the purchase and walked out of the store with a beaming smile on her face.

She rubbed her eyes to brush the slumber away and tied her bathrobe with a quick knot, then started looking around for that knife. The slot in the wooden block had never been empty since the day she'd bought the knives, except when that razor-sharp blade was slicing and dicing at her pleasure.

The knife was nowhere in sight.

Not in the dishwasher.

Not on the counter.

Not on the cutting board.

Not even in the fridge. She checked there last, because there had never been an instance she could remember when any of them might've left a knife in the fridge. They weren't that old yet.

Then she remembered why she'd come downstairs in the dead of the night, and her frown deepened.

She filled a glass with tap water and drank it thirstily, then checked the living room. The TV was off, and Brent wasn't dozing on the couch, the way he did sometimes when he couldn't sleep.

These days, both of them struggled falling asleep. For Gayle, it was as if her body got tired of doing what it was told. After endlessly long days on her feet, working full shifts at the hospital as a surgical nurse then catering to the many whims of her young sons, it refused to find rest, to let her heavy eyelids fall and shield her weary brain from the world and savor a few hours of deep sleep.

With her medical training, she knew what prolonged sleep deprivation was doing to her body, and before long she'd asked one of the doctors to prescribe her a sleeping pill she could take on a regular basis without risking addiction. She'd promised to have herself checked out, do some bloodwork, and find out if there were any underlying causes for her now chronic insomnia, but every day something happened that kept her from taking the elevator down two floors and letting the phlebotomist poke her with a 21-gauge needle.

She was afraid of what the bloodwork would reveal. She was afraid the doctor would find something terrible that meant her life would end before she'd have a chance to enjoy it. Or there would be nothing that serious, just early signs of aging, of becoming a middle-aged woman, of standing in the waiting room of her golden years, or whatever the heck they called it when bodies started falling apart at the seams.

She was only thirty-three, and her fears were premature and irrational. She kept telling herself that, while postponing the lab tests and counting on pills to get some much-needed rest.

She'd taken them as prescribed for a couple of weeks before giving them up. They were top-notch, expensive, the best the industry had to offer for chronic idiopathic insomnia. But she hated how they made her feel in the morning—sluggish, as if walking through water. As if her brain was dosed in marmalade, sticky, heavy, unable to function for the best part of the morning. On top of that, the miracle drug had knocked her lights out within seconds the first night she took it, but then her body started getting used to it, needing more and more time to find repose, and soon needing more and more pills. Not a good outcome.

The night before, she hadn't taken any, deciding that if she was going to toss and turn until her husband woke up and moved downstairs grumbling, she could do that on her own, without the aid of a chemical that would render her a zombie for half the next morning. She'd caught all of two-and-a-half hours of sleep, then woke up about two in the morning and stared at the ceiling.

After an hour of studying the patterns on the ceiling, she'd come downstairs to look for Brent, to tell him he should take the bedroom, because she was going to make herself some chamomile tea and stream an episode or two of *Friends*.

The first thing she noticed was the missing knife, and then she realized that Brent was missing too.

He wasn't in the living room, sleeping on the couch. He wasn't secretly working on his laptop in the downstairs den. He wasn't in the basement workshop either. Maybe he was in the garage, tinkering with the carburetor on his Mustang GT Fastback.

She opened the garage door. She turned on the light and squinted.

Her minivan was missing. The Mustang was still there. And Brent never drove the Odyssey, having nothing but disdain for the reliable workhorse covered in cookie crumbs and littered with toys. He'd dubbed it the Matmobile, a nickname inspired from Batman but twisted to bring a condescending flavor of maternity. He kept saying he was too young to be seen in one, and never once missed the opportunity to say that condoms prevented minivans. That statement always made her cringe a little, wondering if he'd wanted the boys in the first place. Then she'd shrug her doubts away; Brent loved his kids. Next time she'd get a different vehicle. She should've listened.

What in the world had possessed Brent to drive the Matmobile? And where the hell was he, anyway, at three-thirty in the morning? How come she hadn't heard him leave? The garage door opener creaked and groaned loudly, as if the storm-grade, double door was about to get twisted and torn each time someone pressed the remote button.

She looked up at the opener and saw the rope was pulled and the chain disengaged; Brent had opened and then closed the door by hand after he'd pulled out.

Her husband had wanted her oblivious to his outing.

And the knife was missing.

A chill prickled her skin and raised her hairs a little, as if a wave of cold air had engulfed her in a deathly grip. Stunned, she walked inside the kitchen after turning off the light in the garage and closing the door. She reached for another glass of water while memories invaded her like pieces of a puzzle that fit together really well.

There were times when she'd thought she'd left things slightly different from how she'd found them. The radio station setting on her car's sound system. The box of tissues, which was her key weapon in the fight against runny noses, moved out of reach. The position of the steering wheel. She was a creature of habit, maybe more than other people; she always took the slight turn into the garage the same way, and never straightened the wheels after stopping, because it was so much easier to exit the garage in the exact same way she'd entered it.

But Brent was a stickler for order, sometimes compulsive even, and he always straightened the wheels before stopping. She remembered she'd found the wheels on her Odyssey straight a few times because she'd almost backed into the fence, rushed as always to drop the boys at daycare before her shift started. She'd blamed it on her own scattered mind, never once suspecting Brent of driving it while she slept. He would've never touched the Matmobile, not on his life.

Or would he?

More pieces of the same puzzle started to fall into place, and she hated the image they were starting to form. Brent's increasingly gloomy moods of late. His escalating demands in the bedroom, shifting what they were doing together further away from the idea of lovemaking and closer to the unwanted thought that she was being used to satisfy unusual cravings, fantasies she didn't want to begin to understand or imagine. His secretive behavior sometimes risked kindling her jealousy. She'd wondered on occasions if he was seeing another woman but didn't want to believe it. Didn't want her fairy tale to be over, although she knew it was far from a fairy tale these days and closer than ever to an unhappy ending.

When was the last time he'd said a kind word to her? Or held her hand?

She shook her head and wiped an unwanted tear from her eye with a frozen, hastened finger. She stared at the empty spot where the seven-inch blade knife was supposed to spend the night, after she washed and rinsed it by hand to preserve its sharpness.

Gone.

She tried desperately to find innocent reasons why Brent could've driven off in the dead of the night in her minivan, armed with her Santoku knife. She came up empty and frustrated to the point of tears. There was no plausible explanation she could think of.

Then another thought ripped through her consciousness, searing like a thunderbolt. One name came to her mind, and she had to grab the edge of the counter with both hands, gasping, struggling to maintain her balance on her trembling legs.

Ella Fitzpatrick.

The thirteen-year-old girl next door, who had vanished ten days ago, and whose body was just found at the edge of the woods, mutilated and repeatedly stabbed.

With a large, non-serrated knife, the news reporter said.

Just like her Santoku blade.

The sounds of her own gasping breaths startled her.

"No, no, no," she whispered in a panic, desperately thinking what to do.

How could she test her awful suspicions? How could she ask the man she'd married seven years ago if he was the rapist and killer of the little girl who used to live next door? He couldn't be... just couldn't. He must have some explanation for everything, one she'd soon hear with a deep sigh of relief. Then she'd have to live with the shame of doubting him.

She closed her eyes, scrunching her eyelids together, as if to reject an image she didn't want to see, no matter the cost. Against the darkness of her closed eyelids, memories flurried, snippets of life she'd witnessed, moments she'd never paid enough attention to before.

Her husband's smile stretching whenever Ella came outside to play. The way he sat in the armchair by the window, watching her, feigning absentmindedness from behind the white sheers. The way he ran his fingers against her face when he saw her on the sidewalk; apparently innocent, almost parental, yet she'd never seen him ruffle any other kid's hair or pinch any other girl's cheeks but hers.

Ella's.

"Oh, no," she whispered, while tears rolled down her heated face, staining the fabric of her robe.

But then she heard a faint noise. The garage door was being opened slowly, silently, by hand.

Brent was back.

Her heart thumped against her chest, suffocating her, sending her mind in a swirl of panicked thoughts.

Did he see her? Did he notice the light was on?

No, they always left the light on in the kitchen overnight.

Maybe he didn't see her, since she'd been standing close to the door leading to the garage. That corner was tucked behind the fridge, out of sight away from the window.

What should she do?

She looked desperately left and right like a terrified gazelle about to bolt, pressing her hands against her chest to quiet the deafening sound of her beating heart.

Should she confront him?

What if her suspicions were founded? What if the worst nightmare she'd ever had was real?

What if it wasn't?

She snuck inside the pantry and closed the door gently, moments before Brent entered the kitchen, coming from the garage. She held her breath, feeling him near, so near she was afraid he'd sense her body heat, hear her short gasps for the air that couldn't fill her lungs.

She heard a clattering noise when he dropped the knife on the counter. Then she heard footfalls descending into the basement. She listened for a long moment, but heard nothing. Then she heard the pipes moan lightly; the washer was filling with water.

Brent was doing laundry.

At four forty-five in the morning.

She listened, unable, unwilling to move. He took a shower downstairs, a short one. It couldn't've lasted more than five minutes, time in which she couldn't bring herself to go back upstairs and climb into bed. She needed answers more than she needed to feel safe. She knew the moment he'd get to the bedroom and find her gone, he'd rush back downstairs, looking for her.

She'd have the answer she was looking for, ready or not.

When he left the basement and started climbing the stairs toward the second floor, she eased out of the pantry and gently closed the door behind her. She looked for the knife and found it on the counter. Forgetting her earlier plan to lie down on the couch and pretend to be dozing there, she picked it up with both hands, studying it closely.

"Are you looking for something?" Brent said, so close to her she felt his breath on her skin.

Startled, she dropped the knife. It clattered loudly on the floor tiles while she took a step back.

"You scared me," she whispered, choked.

He bent and picked up the knife with a natural gesture. He seemed at ease, his normal self, albeit a little scrutinizing.

"Why are you up?" he asked. "Still can't sleep?"

"Uh-huh," she replied, nodding a couple of times as if to add emphasis to her statement. "I mean, no, I can't sleep."

He gave her the knife, and she took it with trembling fingers. She felt like dropping it into the kitchen sink, unwilling to touch it, as if it burned her skin, Just the thought that her knife had cut into the flesh of—

She shuddered.

"Um, what did you need it for?" she managed to ask, her need for answers overcoming her fears.

"Late-night snack," he lied, without skipping a beat.

Gayle looked at him for a moment, while despair clutched iron fingers around her heart. It couldn't be true. She must've misunderstood. *Oh, God, please...*

"Did you like it?" she asked.

"What?" he replied, unscrewing the cap off a sparkling water bottle.

"The way it cuts," she said, her voice trembling a little. "You didn't like these knives that much when I bought them, remember?"

"Nah, they're good," he replied casually. "They cut really well," he added with a smile.

She forced some air into her lungs.

"When did you wake up?" she asked, hoping for the truth against all reason. "I dozed off downstairs for a while and didn't hear you come down."

"Just a few minutes ago," he replied, smiling at her and

looking her straight in the eye. "Want to go back upstairs? Try for another nap? I'm beat."

She needed more time. She couldn't go upstairs with him, not now, not with so many terrible questions swarming through her mind. Not when she knew something unspeakable was happening. She weighed her options quickly, her training as a surgical nurse coming into play. If healthcare professionals learned something really well on the job, it was making decisions quickly based on critical, objective data. The time for being weak and scared had long come and gone.

"It's almost five-thirty," she replied calmly, putting the knife back in its block. "In forty minutes that damn alarm will go off, and I'd rather not do that to myself." She turned and smiled at him. "Why don't I make us a cup of coffee, get an early start to the day?"

He frowned a little, rubbing his fingers against his chin stubble. "Will you?" he asked, sounding uncertain.

"You bet," she replied, grabbing the coffee pot and filling it with water from the tap. "What would you like? Java? French vanilla?" As she went through the familiar motions and phrases, she found it easier to pretend everything was fine.

"Let's do Java today," he replied, a little more relaxed apparently. "We didn't get much sleep; we're going to need it."

"You got it," she replied, pressing the button.

Water sizzled against the heating elements as the coffee maker started to brew. She grabbed two clean mugs from the cupboard and headed toward the living room.

"Come on, we'll watch the morning news together, just like old times," she said, smiling widely.

He followed hesitantly, but eventually sat on the couch leaning against the armrest. Gayle put the two mugs down on the glass surface of the coffee table, then went to the kitchen and brought back a couple of coasters. She turned on the TV and they watched Matthew McConaughey in a Lincoln commercial, inexplicably rubbing his fingers and talking to a bull.

"Why the hell does he do that?" Brent asked. "And why is he turning around and leaving? What's the message here?"

They laughed, and, for a moment, life seemed to be normal again.

A few minutes later, the coffee machine beeped and that illusion of normality vanished. She went back to the kitchen.

"Cream and sugar?" she asked, although she already knew the answer.

"Cream on the side," he replied, laughter still tainting his voice.

She fussed around the pot for a while, keeping her eyes on Brent. Only the tip of his head was visible from the kitchen, but he seemed engulfed in the morning show, relaxed, leaning against the backrest.

She opened the upper cupboard they used as a medicine cabinet and slipped out one blister pack of pills. One by one, she removed a few sleeping pills from the pack, piercing the metallic membranes with her fingernail, careful not to make a noise. She stirred the pills into the coffee pot and thankfully they dissolved quickly. They were almost tasteless; she remembered their chalk-like taste on her tongue, a little bitter.

Finally, she drained most of the cream into the sink until only a spoonful remained.

"Touch of hazelnut?" she asked.

"Yeah," he replied, not taking his eyes off the TV.

She added the flavoring, knowing it would cover any trace of unfamiliar taste and went back into the living room, carrying the pot and the creamer on a small tray she set in front of Brent.

"Do the honors, please."

He poured her coffee first, then his. She poured the last remaining cream in her mug, and only added a drop or two to his cup. Cream had an unwanted effect on sleep medication; it coated the chemical, rendering it less effective, and she needed his to work as fast as possible.

"Sorry, honey, we're out," she said, shaking the carton to try to conjure another drop.

He waved her apology away and took a big sip.

"It's good," he said, as he leaned back against the couch.

She nested her mug in her hands, blowing against the wisps of steam, inhaling the hazelnut aroma. She took a small sip and waited, pretending to care about the military maneuvers in Afghanistan.

"Can't believe these guys," Brent commented. Then he looked at her and a slight frown wrinkled his brow. "Aren't you drinking yours?"

"Uh-huh, yeah," she replied, and then took a big gulp that burned her tongue. "Ouch," she reacted, sticking her tongue out and laughing quietly. She wasn't feeling any effects yet, but she was used to the pills and she'd added cream. While the new segment of ads started running, she found herself doing some math in her head.

She'd added about nine pills to a coffee pot that held three mugs of coffee, maybe three and a half. If he drank half of his, he'd fall asleep in about ten minutes. If he drank it all, he'd be out like a light.

"Cheers," she gestured, raising the coffee cup and taking another sip. "Soon I'll have to wake the boys, and all peace on earth will vanish."

As if remembering their morning routine claimed all the energy he had left, Brent raised his mug and drank as if it were water. "Yeah, almost there," he reacted, wiping his mouth with the back of his hand. "But we still have some time," he added, a bit slurred.

She waited, not daring to move, until his breathing became regular and light, and a barely audible snore moved his lower lip with every breath. Then she jumped to her feet and rushed into the kitchen.

Without hesitation, she leaned over the edge of the sink and plunged two fingers down her throat. Instantly, she started retching, her stomach expelling most of the spiked coffee she'd ingested. Once her stomach settled, she checked on Brent again, but he was fast asleep. His cup was empty. He was going to be out cold for a while.

But she couldn't risk it. First, she rushed into the garage, where she found a bunch of cable ties. She returned to the living room and ziptied his ankles, and then his wrists. He shifted in his sleep, giving her a start, but he didn't wake up.

Then she started searching. She didn't know what she was searching for, only that she'd know it when she'd found it. She inspected the knife closely but didn't see any traces of blood on it. That didn't mean there wasn't any; it just meant she didn't see it, and that meant her most burning question was still unanswered.

She went to the basement and looked through the clothes that were spinning in the washer. She powered down the machine and pulled the shirt out, inspecting it closely under the dim light of the laundry room. She thought she saw a stain that could've been blood; she wasn't sure, so she squeezed the water out of the shirt and hung it to dry. Then she inspected his pants; the left leg had a brownish blot, and the simple sight of that stain and the implications of its origins made her feel like throwing up again.

Unaware she was whimpering, she climbed back to the main floor to his office and went through his laptop, his cell phone, his desk drawers. She didn't find anything incriminating, but the more she searched, the more she knew, instinctively, that she was getting close, that she was going to find the evidence she was looking for.

She closed the last desk drawer and sighed, not ready to give up. Brent spent lots of time seated at that desk, reading, researching, working on his laptop. Looking outside. The office window had a prime view of the Fitzpatrick family's backyard.

That's where he'd watched Ella play, day after day.

"No," she whispered, "no, no, please, no."

Angry, she pulled the drawers out of the desk, one by one. Then she saw it, a tiny object wrapped in plastic and taped against the back of the desk. With trembling hands, she reached out and almost touched it, but then thought better and rushed to the kitchen to get latex gloves before removing it.

Carefully, she unwrapped the plastic and exposed a girl's locket on a fine, silver chain. She opened the locket and found inside the photos of Ella's parents.

Her knees gave out, and she fell to the floor, sobbing. She recalled the news piece when the police had identified Ella's body and said that a unique pendant was missing, probably a keepsake the murderer had added to his collection.

Yes, collection, she repeated to herself, the word sending renewed shivers down her spine.

Because the FBI had said that little Ella Fitzpatrick had died at the hands of a serial killer, an unknown person suspected in several other murders.

She retched again, but found the strength to continue tearing the desk apart, drawer by drawer. She didn't dare remove the other packets she'd found taped to the wooden desk; with each new find, a piece of her heart was dying.

She pulled away from the desk and took her phone out of her bathrobe pocket. Her vision blurred with tears, and her fingers were frozen and shaking. She had to try three times to get the number right, until she could hear a voice say, "Nine-one-one, what's your emergency?"

When the police officers arrived, she opened the door and let them inside. She couldn't say a single word, nor could she cry any more tears. She just pointed toward the man snoring on the couch, a man she thought she'd known like the back of her hand. A stranger. A murderer.

While the police and crime scene technicians took over the house, Gayle kept her eyes focused on a patch of perfectly blue sky, right above the lush green of the front yard oak tree. It was time to wake the boys and take them to her mother's, before the media showed up. It was time to call the hospital and tell them she wouldn't be coming in today.

It was time to grieve.

She breathed in the fresh morning air and thought about the sleeping pills she'd swallowed, dissolved in that coffee, the last thing she'd shared with her husband. She should've been sleepy, drowsy from the little bit she'd ingested, but she was wide awake. Nothing but awake, all senses alert, all her wits about her, ready to pounce, ready to fight. Ready to face life as a single mother, as the soon-to-be-stigmatized wife of a serial killer.

But at least now she was awake.

CHARDONNAY

He watched the suspect through the two-way mirror for a few minutes, planning the conversation. The woman was calm and composed, albeit a little sad, but otherwise unfazed by the fact that she'd been sitting by herself in a police interrogation room for more than an hour.

Arlene Banks knew they had nothing on her.

Sure, her husband, John, was having an affair with a much younger woman, the twenty-two-year-old Diane Grenier, but he'd been discreet about it, only meeting at her home, during business hours, when Arlene believed he was meeting with clients at his accounting firm. There wasn't a single shred of evidence to prove Arlene even knew about the affair.

As for the cause of death, the medical examiner had refused to write down suspicious circumstances. The bodies were found in an eternal embrace, in Diane's bed, without a single trace of evidence to speak of foul play. They'd died in their sleep, peacefully, from carbon monoxide emanating from a poorly maintained fireplace. Typical case of bad luck—even the CO detector had been installed without a power backup, and the batteries had outlived their usefulness.

Was it really bad luck?

In his entire career of almost twenty years as a Seattle detective, Max Whitner had never been more certain of anything. Somehow, against all evidence, he believed Arlene Banks had killed her cheating husband and his mistress. All he had to do was get her to confess. But why the hell would she do that?

The only thing he had going for him was that the widow hadn't lawyered up yet. She sat there calmly, sniffling on occasions, but not pacing as an innocent person might in those circumstances. However, she'd been told the police needed some questions answered, nothing to worry about, and she'd volunteered to come down to the precinct for the conversation. Just as a guiltless, grieving widow would. He still got nothing; he was grasping at straws.

He grabbed the case file and went inside the room, still undecided which way to take the conversation. The sergeant had given him until noon to wrap it up, in the absence of a suspicious-circumstances finding from the ME and any shred of physical evidence. Still, he wasn't ready to let it go just yet.

He greeted Arlene Banks politely and thanked her for coming in.

She nodded, accepting his thanks. "Let's get this over with, Detective. As you can imagine, these are trying times for me, for my family."

Hesitating a little, he extracted a crime scene photo, showing the two victims in their naked embrace, and placed it in front of the grieving widow.

She promptly turned away, closing her tearful eyes and letting out a subdued cry of pain. "Please," she whimpered, "no more."

Hoping he was right about the widow, and that his many years on the job hadn't turned him into a completely heartless bastard, he insisted. "Please, Mrs. Banks, I need to ask you again. Have you ever seen this woman before?"

"No," she said, squeezing her eyes shut. "Never. John's affair was a complete surprise to me. Who was she?"

"An intern at his firm, fresh out of college," he replied matter-of-factly. "These things happen, Mrs. Banks. An older man, maybe going through some kind of midlife crisis, meets an attractive, young woman who doesn't say no. Was he?"

She opened her swollen eyes and looked straight at him. "Was he, what?"

"Going through midlife crisis."

She shook her head and let it hang. "No, I didn't think so. Our sons have both moved out, they're with their own families now. It was just John and me, growing old in an empty house, but he seemed okay about it."

"He was fifty-three years old," the detective said. "How long had you two been married?"

"Almost thirty years," she replied quietly, in a choked whisper.

Whitner realized he was going nowhere with that line of questioning and shifted gears.

"There were no messages on your husband's phone," he said. "Nothing to attest to their relationship."

She patted her nose with a tissue and looked at him, probably waiting for a question.

"The technicians discovered they were using an app that deleted the messages the moment they were read."

She closed her eyes again. "He wasn't secretive with his phone in my presence. He didn't lock it, and I—"

"You thought he was honest?" he interrupted, instantly wishing he hadn't.

"Yes. I never worried about him cheating. He... was an honest man. At least, that's what I thought."

"You reported him missing when he didn't come home last Friday night," he stated. "How did you know he wasn't in a meeting, or out for drinks with his coworkers?"

"He was never that late. I waited..." she explained, and then covered her mouth with her hands, as if to hold a heavy sob captive.

"Do you know how we located him, Mrs. Banks?" he asked quietly.

"No."

"Our technical team tracked down his phone to Miss Grenier's address. These things," he said, gesturing toward the iPhone sealed inside an evidence bag, "can be located with an accuracy of a few feet. Amazing."

Sometime in the past few seconds, Mrs. Banks had stopped crying. Her tears had dried, and the expression in her eyes was one of focus, of alertness. People's brains aren't that great at multitasking when it comes to basic, primal functions, like grieving and being vigilant at the same time. He was on the right track.

"You know what else we discovered on your husband's phone, Mrs. Banks?"

She shook her head but didn't say a word. Lines of tension developed in her jaw, in the way her hands were clasped, in the ridges on her forehead.

"There was an app on his phone, one that enables a regular user, like you, for example, to track his phone with the same level of accuracy as our technicians can. All the user needs is to have the same app installed on his or her phone, and bam! They can stalk their prey without them ever suspecting."

She didn't move a muscle, and, based on what he was observing, didn't even breathe.

"It must have been painful as hell, Mrs. Banks, to find out your husband was spending countless hours at that address. Jealousy burns deep inside one's heart; suffocates one with unspeakable anger. I bet you drove there one day and waited, patiently, until you could see who lived at that address."

"I have no idea what you're talking about. I've never, um, stalked that woman in my life."

He stopped for a second, thinking. She sounded truthful and seemed a bit more relaxed. But how else could she have learned Diane's identity? Like everything else she did, remotely, using technology.

"You didn't, that's right. You did a reverse search on that address, and instantly knew everything there was to know about the beautiful Diane Grenier, didn't you?"

A flicker of rage sparkled in Arlene's eyes, before she could contain it behind batting eyelashes.

"It must have been awful to see her face, to see how young she was, to realize that what you had and lost could never be recovered," he said, speaking slowly, quietly. He almost sympathized with her; he understood her pain but didn't agree with her actions. "Your youth, the best years of your life," he continued, "spent on a man who turned his back on you and went out there, looking for someone younger."

She leaned against the back of her chair and pressed her lips together.

"If I were you," he continued, "I don't know what I'd've done. I would've strangled the bitch, or something. But he was just as much to blame as she was, right?"

She didn't reply, and her eyes had stopped shooting fiery glances. "I think it's about time we end this conversation, Detective. I'm not sure what you're looking for, but I can't give it to you."

She stood with ease and ran her hands against her jacket, straightening it, and then arranged the collar of her silk blouse.

"Just a few more minutes, if I may?" he pleaded. "Don't you want to know what happened next?"

She didn't react, and he continued, unfazed. "No, you don't, because you already know, don't you? May I take a look at your cell phone? Just to rule you out?"

"You'll need a warrant for that," she replied. "My phone is very personal."

"Neighbors said they saw someone a few weeks earlier working on the chimney," he continued. "That someone, instead of cleaning it, must have planted the bird's nest that was to blame for CO accumulating in the house. Then that someone waited for a fire to be started in the fireplace. One thing I don't know was how the batteries were replaced in the CO detector. How did that person gain access to the house?"

"Detective, if you continue along these lines, I'm going to have to ask to have my lawyer present. I don't want to be the victim of a fishing expedition."

"No need for that, if you won't be answering any questions. Before you leave, just one more minute, if you could hear me out."

She nodded once, but took three steps toward the door. He didn't stop her. Instead, he stood and approached her a little more, then looked her in the eye from up close.

"Technology can do amazing things these days. We can track your phone's GPS history, for example, and put you at Diane Grenier's address at least once, when you tampered with the CO detector, maybe the same day you planted the bird's nest in the chimney," he said, showing nothing but confidence, despite the fact that phone GPS tracking was nowhere near what people expected it to be. Mrs. Banks didn't flinch.

"It will probably put you at that location months before they died," he continued, and thought he saw a flicker in her eyes, just a quick dilation in her pupils. "How was it, waiting for your husband to die, knowing that every day he went to see her could be his last? Did that make you feel good, Mrs. Banks? Did that wash away a little of that scorching jealousy? Did you feel avenged? Was it intoxicating, maybe?"

There it was—a flare in her nostrils, her chin thrust forward.

"I bet you felt really good, knowing the cheating bastard had it coming, any day. If I were you, I would've spent each lonely evening with a beer in my hand, just anticipating, visualizing, feeling vindicated. Because it must sting like crazy to be replaced like that, thrown to the curb like an old shoe, like nothing."

Her lips twitched, as if they wanted to articulate some words, but her willpower kept them under control.

"What was it, Mrs. Banks? Beer? Bourbon?"

A long moment went by, while their eyes were locked together without flinching, without a blink. Whitner managed to convey understanding, empathy for the abandoned woman, and it showed in his eyes. He understood. He probably was the only one who did.

"Chardonnay," she whispered, and then sat down. "It was Chardonnay."

ADAM

Raindrops rapped against the cardboard, forcing him to wake up. He groaned and cursed, then turned on his side, pulling a bundle of rags under his head into a makeshift pillow. He didn't mind the rain; not anymore. He'd found some heavy-duty vapor barrier in a trash can by the local Home Depot store, and he'd used it to insulate his provisional abode, tucked against a brick wall behind the old dairy factory, now closed.

Other than rain and the distant rumbling of traffic on the nearby street, no sound bothered the relative peace and quiet of the back alley. He was the only tenant in the area, drifters and street bums knowing better than to come near him. He didn't want company; he'd made it abundantly clear to anyone who'd crossed his path.

If he couldn't see the people who mattered, he didn't want to see anyone else. And he couldn't see them anymore, not unless there was an afterlife, and someone would have the mercy to put him out of his misery. Soon. The sooner, the better. Not nearly soon enough.

Against his eyelids, squeezed shut to block any trace of daylight, he could see their shapes catching form, becoming real, like a movie watched through a distant, foggy window. If he listened hard enough, he could hear them laughing in the gentle, warm rain, dancing barefoot in the grass of their suburban home. He could hear them squealing happily as the rain had started to fall harder, soaking them but not chasing them back inside.

Then it all went away, in one of those sudden moments when too much happiness triggers the rage of the gods above, or whatever pretense of meaning one could find in the words, "freak accident."

He knew better; there was no secret, cathartic meaning hidden behind such words; only a game of chance, the roaring laughter of a pissed-off fate that had it out for him. He'd delivered many next-of-kin notifications after such accidents, after random murders on the city streets, enough to know there was nothing to follow after that. No closure, no recovery, no life. Nothing but waiting in line for the Grim Reaper to catch a moment and pluck him out of the ranks of the living, fixing the mistake he'd made when he let them go shopping alone that Sunday.

The sound of a kid's voice resounded in his mind, crystalline, yet terrified.

"Mommy?" the high-pitched voice called.

He frowned; the voice didn't resemble the one he cherished in his memories. It wasn't his son's, reverberating across years to fill the abyss in his heart. He pulled the makeshift cardboard door to the side a little and looked outside.

A tall, blonde woman crouched, to be on the same eye level with the little girl, and gently tucked a strand of rebel hair behind her ear. She held an umbrella above their heads and had pushed her daughter against the wall, covering the child with her own body, keeping her out of passersby's sight.

"It's okay, baby," the woman said, sniffling and quickly running her fingers against her cheeks to make her tears disappear. "We'll be okay. Let me call your aunt; she'll help us."

He groaned and let himself fall back against the musty wall. As much as he hated strangers in his forsaken corner of the world, he wasn't about to scare those two away and add to their misery. He sighed quietly, decided to wait them out. They'd be on their way soon.

A trace of who he used to be came to the forefront of his mind, uninvited, and started poking him with questions. What were those two scared of, and what were they doing in that part of town? They looked well-dressed, enough to expect they'd travel in a car, or at least a cab. No one decent walked anymore, not on those streets anyway.

"Hey, it's me," he heard the woman say.

He peeked from behind the cardboard wall and saw her speaking into her phone, while looking at the street with watchful eyes filled with terror.

"He's coming after me," the woman continued, barely above a whisper, to keep her daughter from hearing. "He took my car; we're on foot. I didn't want to take a cab from the apartment in case he had me watched. But he's coming, I can feel it."

A few seconds of silence ensued, relative silence against the sound of the cold rain falling incessantly from the dark, gray skies. Whoever was at the other end of that phone call was probably giving the young woman instructions.

Then he heard her gasp and whimper, "He found us... help me, please, call somebody," she pleaded, her voice louder, pleading, terrified.

He peeked at the street and saw a black Cadillac Escalade come to a stop in front of the two. Three men climbed out of that car and rushed at the woman, who started screaming.

"No, no," she pleaded, hiding her daughter behind her back.

He clenched his fists but decided to wait another moment, seeing the nine-millimeter handguns the goons were packing. Not that he feared death; not at all. What he feared was getting shot before he could take them all out. Any one of those three were more than enough to overpower the young woman and her daughter.

Where were the damn cops when you needed them?

Two of the men grabbed the little girl and put her in the back seat of the Escalade, ignoring her kicks and screams. They were careful not to harm her, but firm at the same time.

The third man, a bulky forty-something with a trimmed

beard and a bunch of tattoos, grabbed the woman by the collar and slammed her hard against the wall.

"You piece of shit, you think you can run away from me?" he growled, glaring at her from only a few inches away. "You're never going to see your kid again, you stupid whore," he added, shoving her once again against the wall.

Then he turned away, not before spitting at the woman's feet, and climbed in the passenger seat of the Cadillac. He slammed the door shut and rolled down the window, then leaned back in the seat and took a sip from a paper cup bearing a nearby coffee shop's logo.

The woman let out a heart-wrenching wail, then found more strength in that tiny body of hers and raised her fist in the air. "I'll never stop fighting you, Boris, you hear me? You son of a bitch, I swear I'll come after you, if it's the last thing I do."

The man she'd called Boris hurled the cup at the woman and laughed when the liquid splashed on impact against her face. "There, bitch, I just doubled your street value."

Then the Cadillac disappeared, roars of laughter cascading through the SUV's open windows, almost completely obliterating the little girl's sobs and cries for her mother.

The woman let herself slide against the wall, probably too weak to stand and too drained to care about the puddle of water at her feet. Sobbing, she crouched against the wall, hugging her knees. A few yards away, the wind carried the umbrella away toward the park.

He crawled out of his improvised shelter and ran to catch the thing, then brought it to her without a word. When she realized someone was standing next to her, she was startled.

"Please," she whispered, "don't hurt me. I have some money."

He held his hand in the air, refusing the offer, handing her the umbrella. "I don't need your money," he said, the sound of his own voice strange to him after so much silence. "I'm not here to hurt you."

He leaned over and carefully picked up the coffee cup, using a small piece of paper to grab it. Then he studied it attentively, squinting in the dim light. Satisfied with what he saw, he turned to her.

"Who was that man?" he asked, crouching next to her.

The woman's tears returned, and she turned her face away, ashamed. "My ex-husband," she whispered.

"What does he do for a living?"

"Real estate," she replied. "Some other stuff too, but he won't say."

He listened to her speak; her English was clear, her accent pure American northeast. She wasn't Russian; at least not born and raised over there, like Boris had sounded.

"Why?" she asked, looking at him with a faint glimmer of hope.

"Did you see that star tattoo on his chest? The one that looks like a compass rose?"

She nodded and swallowed hard.

"That's Bratva, the Russian mob," he announced calmly. "Based on the location and the size of that ink job, your ex-husband is a top player in the Jersey Russian mob."

She covered her gaping mouth with her hand in a quick, startled gesture.

"What, you didn't know?" he reacted. "He's done time," he added, thinking of the prison tats that adorned the man's hands.

"All that was before we met," she replied quietly. "I had suspicions, but he swore to me he was legit. I... wanted to believe him."

He stood and extended a grimy hand, inviting her to stand. She took his hand without hesitation, glancing at the coffee cup he shielded cautiously from the rain, holding it close to the wall, where the roof above extended some protection.

"You wouldn't have a plastic bag, would you?" he asked.

She hesitated for a moment, then reached inside her purse and fished out a Ziploc bag holding some candy. She emptied the bag and gave it to him, watching every move he made with curious eyes, yet not daring to ask.

He sealed the cup in the bag and slid it inside the pocket of his ratty jacket.

"How did you manage to leave him?" he asked.

She looked sideways for a moment, then straight at him. "I served him divorce papers and a restraining order at the same time, with my lawyer present," she said, and a trace of pride tinged her voice. "I thought I was being smart. Then I took him to court and got sole custody of Brianna." Her voice broke when she spoke her daughter's name.

"What's your name?" he asked.

"Jennifer," she replied, extending her hand.

He hesitated a little, then shook it briefly. "You were very brave to leave your husband. I bet it wasn't easy. I bet life with him wasn't either."

Tears flooded her eyes again. "He took my daughter," she said, "and I'll never see her again."

"Don't worry," he replied, "I think I can handle him."

"You?" she reacted, sizing him up.

He let a crooked smile stretch his lips unevenly. "I don't look like much these days, do I?" he mumbled. He was scrawny and pale, and only here and there traces of muscle still covered his bones, a far cry from the state's close quarters combat champion he'd been crowned only five years ago.

"I meant no disrespect," she whispered. "Let me apologize by getting us some breakfast."

He smiled again. "Thanks, but I'd rather take care of some business first. Tell me, where would I find this ex-husband of yours?"

"He's got a building downtown, on Newark Avenue, above

a Russian restaurant," she said, "but he's got his people with him all the time. They'll kill you..." She hesitated for a moment, then continued, "Sorry, I didn't get your name."

He ignored her question. He couldn't bear the thought of hearing his name spoken out loud by this stranger, overriding the voices he kept hearing in his mind. Instead, he grabbed her elbow and led her to the coffee shop across the street.

"Wait for me here," he said. "Something tells me things are about to get better."

Then he turned away and headed for the subway with a spring in his step.

Thirty minutes later, he landed on the doorstep of a Russian eatery, on the ground floor of a five-story brick building, probably one of those old manufacturing facilities that had been converted to lofts.

He entered the restaurant calmly, his arms relaxed alongside his body, ready to pounce at the slightest sign of aggression.

"Get the hell outta here," a man snapped from behind the bar.

"I'm here to see Boris," he announced.

"I don't know of any Boris," the man replied, then reached under the counter and produced a baseball bat.

"Oh, well," he replied calmly. "He's going to get arrested in a couple of hours. He'll be terribly disappointed to hear you had the opportunity to let me give him a heads-up but decided otherwise."

The bat disappeared, but the man still scrutinized him with fierce eyes. After a long moment, he came out from behind the counter and opened a door leading to some stairs.

"After you," he invited the bartender with a firm voice. The man obliged.

Moments later, he was led into a large room, furnished with pieces that seemed to have been picked up at garage sales or some thrift store. Brianna sat on a weathered leather sofa, whimpering, while a man stood next to her, watching her closely. The man kept his arms crossed at his chest, but that didn't hide the double gun harness he wore under his jacket, nor his well-developed biceps.

Another two men stood next to a desk covered with paperwork and dirty glasses. From behind that desk, Boris shot the bartender an aggravated glare. "Who the hell is this hobo? He's stinking up the place."

"He says he's got info, boss," he replied, then scurried away downstairs.

Boris stared at his visitor incredulously. "Let's hear it."

"You're getting arrested today," he said, glad to see the reaction in the man's pupils. Good; he'd struck a chord.

Boris frowned and stood, then approached him with his fists clenched. "Where did you hear that?"

"Oh, I didn't hear it," the visitor replied, "I'm making it happen."

Boris froze for a split second, then pulled out his gun and trained it on the man's chest. Two of his goons followed suit, while a third grabbed his arms and held them tightly crossed behind his back. He didn't resist, nor did he take his eyes off the Russian's.

Boris gestured, and the third thug let go of his arms and searched his pockets. He found his wallet and opened it, flipping through whatever was left in there.

"Don't insult my intelligence," the visitor replied. "You know I wouldn't be in here, talking to you, without a backup plan."

"He's a cop," the thug said, his voice tinted with a trace of panic. "Or used to be. His ID expired two years ago."

Boris pressed his lips together, anger twisting and scrunching his features. "Talk," he ordered, not lowering his weapon.

"You hurled a coffee cup at your ex-wife this morning," he said calmly, almost with a sense of satisfaction that came across clearly in his voice. "It had your prints and your DNA; you're in the system and you know how this works." He paused for a moment, giving Boris time to catch up. "The morgue is filled with John Does and Jane Does," he continued. "As you can tell, I know my way around dead bodies and crime scene evidence. I see an opportunity here. With little effort, I can throw your ass in jail for murder one."

Boris put his finger on the trigger and started squeezing.

"Unless," the visitor continued unfazed, gesturing toward Brianna, "you return this young lady to her mother's sole custody and you resume alimony payments immediately."

"Who the hell are you, huh? And why the fuck do you care?"

"I'm no one," he laughed bitterly, "but I do care. And I'll be caring for a long time, longer than you'll get to litter this earth."

"Tell me why I shouldn't kill you now," Boris said, inches away from his face.

He could see the Russian's veins pulsing under his skin, the accelerated heart rate of fear. "You know why," he replied simply. "I don't have the incriminating evidence with me," he added, turning his pockets inside out. "Someone else has that coffee cup, and the moment you do anything to piss me off, your DNA will be found on any number of dead bodies currently housed at the city morgue." He grinned. "That's going to hang over your head for as long as you live, you understand me?"

"I will kill you," Boris said coldly. Nevertheless, he lowered his gun and tucked it inside his belt. "One day I will find you and I will kill you, slowly, taking my time, after I've killed everyone you care about. Whatever it is you think you have, I'll find it. Just watch me."

"Sure, knock yourself out," the visitor said, shrugging. "I believe you also need to return the young woman's car. How about a bonus for her inconvenience, say, a hundred grand, to cover her laundry bills? Oh, and your child support payments have doubled, effective immediately."

The Russian clenched his fists so tightly he could hear his joints crack. He remained calm, staring at him with unflinching eyes, ready to die but knowing he wasn't going to yet.

"The more you threaten me, the more your price goes up, and not a dime of it is for me," he announced. "Let's see, a house in the suburbs? A college fund for your daughter?"

Boris turned without a word and snatched a set of car keys from his desk. He beckoned and one of his bodyguards grabbed Brianna by the hand.

Twenty minutes later, the Cadillac stopped at the curb in front of the small coffee shop where Jennifer sat at a table, pale and shivering, waiting. When she saw them, she rushed outside, holding both her hands at her mouth, probably trying to contain a sob.

With a hand gesture, the man stopped Boris from getting out of the SUV, under Jennifer's stunned eyes. "You won't be needed here today. You can go." He watched Boris taking a deep, frustrated breath of air, getting ready to spill a mouthful of threats and curses. "Uh-uh," he said, admonishing him with his finger, "not in front of your daughter."

Then the man got out of the SUV, holding Brianna's hand. Once safely on the sidewalk, he let her run to her mother. The Cadillac vanished quickly, while he watched the little girl hug her mother. He tried to keep his eyes from moistening, even if he could've blamed it on the rain.

How he wished… But, no. Not for him. Not anymore.

He turned to leave, but Jennifer caught his sleeve.

"Thank you," she said, then hugged him tightly, burying her tear-streaked face against his chest. He shuddered, thinking how he must've smelled, but she didn't seem to care.

Gently, he pushed her away; he wasn't ready for any human contact, any warmth. He didn't want to be ready, not ever again. Last time it had cost him too much.

"I'll keep an eye on you two," he said, "check up on you every now and then, to make sure you're okay," he said.

"Come with us," Jennifer said. "Please."

He shook his head, at a loss for words, at least for a few moments. "No... I can't. But I'll be close enough, in case your ex gets any crazy ideas."

A glimpse of fear touched her eyes. "What should I do? Should we move away? My sister has a horse farm in Montana, and we could—"

"No need for that," he replied, starting to dig through the trash can at the corner of the café. "Not unless you want to." He fished out the coffee cup, still intact in its Ziploc bag, and held it up high. "Give me your phone, please."

She obliged without a word.

The man took a photo of the coffee cup as it was, sealed in the bag, then handed her the phone.

"Any time Boris causes you trouble, just text him this photo."

"And say what?" she asked, a deep frown showing her confusion.

"Nothing at all; he'll understand. This picture is worth a thousand words, maybe even more," he added, then turned around and walked away, tucking the evidence deep inside his pocket.

Jennifer rushed after him and stopped him again. "At least tell me your name," she pleaded.

He looked at the two of them, their hands clasped tightly, the little girl hugging her mom's leg every chance she got. Maybe, sometime in the future, there could be another chance for him. Maybe he could learn to let another woman's voice call out his name.

"Adam," he eventually said, his voice choked a little. "My name is Adam."

~The End~

If *Love, Lies, and Murder* had you totally enthralled and gasping at the twists, then you have to read more captivating page-turners by Leslie Wolfe!

Read on for a preview from a best-selling, full-length thriller:

Dawn Girl

**A short-fused FBI Agent who hides a terrible secret. A serial killer you won't see coming.
A heart-stopping race to catch him.**

THANK YOU!

A big, heartfelt thank you for choosing to read my book. If you enjoyed it, please take a moment to leave me a four or five-star review; I would be very grateful. It doesn't need to be more than a couple of words, and it makes a huge difference.

Join my mailing list to receive special offers, exclusive bonus content, and news about upcoming new releases. Use the button below, visit www.LeslieWolfe.com to sign up, or email me at LW@WolfeNovels.com.

Did you enjoy *Love, Lies and Murder*? Would you like to see some of these characters in full-length novels? Which ones? Your thoughts and feedback are very valuable to me. Please contact me directly through one of the channels listed below. Email works best: LW@WolfeNovels.com or use the button below:

CONNECT WITH ME!

Email: LW@WolfeNovels.com
Facebook: https://www.facebook.com/wolfenovels
Follow Leslie on Amazon: http://bit.ly/WolfeAuthor
Follow Leslie on BookBub: http://bit.ly/wolfebb
Website: www.LeslieWolfe.com

Visit Leslie's Amazon store: http://bit.ly/WolfeAll

Preview: Dawn Girl

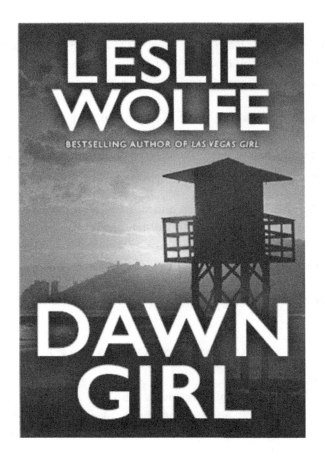

Chapter One

Ready

She made an effort to open her eyes, compelling her heavy eyelids to obey. She swallowed hard, her throat raw and dry, as she urged the wave of nausea to subside. Dizzy and confused, she struggled to gain awareness. Where was she? She felt numb and shaky, unable to move, as if awakening from a deep sleep or a coma. She tried to move her arms, but couldn't. Something kept her immobilized, but didn't hurt her. Or maybe she couldn't feel the pain, not anymore.

Her eyes started to adjust to the darkness, enough to distinguish the man moving quietly in the room. His silhouette flooded her foggy brain with a wave of memories. She gasped, feeling her throat constrict and burning tears rolling down her swollen cheeks.

Her increased awareness sent waves of adrenaline through her body, and she tried desperately to free herself from her restraints. With each useless effort, she panted harder, gasping for air, forcing it into her lungs. Fear put a strong chokehold on her throat and was gaining ground, as she rattled her restraints helplessly, growing weaker with every second. She felt a wave of darkness engulf her, this time the darkness coming from within her weary brain. She fought against that darkness, and battled her own betraying body.

The noises she made got the man's attention.

"I see you're awake. Excellent," the man said, without turning.

She watched him place a syringe on a small, metallic tray. Its handle clinked, followed by another sound, this time the raspy, telling sound of a file cutting through the neck of a glass vial. Then a pop when the man opened the vial. He grabbed the syringe and loaded the liquid from the vial, then carefully removed any air, pushing the piston until several droplets of fluid came out.

Dizziness overtook her, and she closed her eyes for a second.

"Shit," the man mumbled, then opened a drawer and went through it in a hurry.

She felt the needle poke deeply in her thigh, like it was happening to another person. She felt it, but distantly. She perceived a subdued burning sensation where he pushed the fluid into her muscle, then that went away when he pulled the needle out. She closed her weary eyes again, listless against her restraints.

The man cracked open ammonia salts under her nose, and she bounced back into reality at the speed of a lightning strike, aware, alert, and angry. For a second she fought to free herself, but froze when her eyes focused on the man in front of her.

He held a scalpel, close to her face. In itself, the small, shiny, silver object was capable of bringing formidable healing, as well as immense pain. The difference stood in the hand wielding it. She knew no healing was coming her way; only pain.

"No, no, please…" she pleaded, tears falling freely from her puffy eyes, burning as they rolled down her cheeks. "Please, no. I… I'll do anything."

"I am ready," the man said. He seemed calm, composed, and dispassionate. "Are you ready?"

"No, no, please…" she whimpered.

"Yeah," he said softly, almost whispering, inches away from her face. "Please say no to me. I love that."

She fell quiet, scared out of her mind. This time was different. *He* was different.

Chapter Two

Dawn

"What if we get caught?" the girl whispered, trailing behind the boy.

They walked briskly on the small residential street engulfed in darkness, keeping to the middle of the road. There were no sidewalks. High-end homes lined up both sides, most likely equipped with sensor floodlights they didn't want to trip.

She tugged at his hand, but he didn't stop. "You never care about these things, Carl, but I do. If we get caught, I'll be grounded, like, forever!"

The boy kept going, his hand firmly clasping hers.

"Carl!" she raised the pitch in her whisper, letting her anxiety show more.

He stopped and turned, facing her. He frowned a little, seeing her anguish, but then smiled and caressed a loose strand of hair rebelling from under her sweatshirt's hood.

"There's no one, Kris. No one's going to see us. See? No lights are on, nothing. Everyone's asleep. Zee-zee-zee. It's five in the morning."

"I know," she sighed, "but—"

He kissed her pouted lips gently, a little boyish hesitation and awkwardness in his move.

"We'll be okay, I promise," he said, then grabbed her hand again. "We're almost there, come on. You'll love it."

A few more steps and the small street ended into the paved parking lot of what was going to be a future development of sorts, maybe a shopping center. From there, they had to cross

Highway 1. They crouched down near the road, waiting for the light traffic to be completely clear. They couldn't afford to be seen, not even from a distance. At the right moment, they crossed the highway, hand in hand, and cut across the field toward the beach. Crossing Ocean Drive was next, then cutting through a few yards of shrubbery and trees to get to the sandy beach.

"Jeez, Carl," Kris protested, stopping in her tracks at the tree line. "Who knows what creatures live here? There could be snakes. Lizards. Gah…"

"There could be, but there aren't," Carl replied, seemingly sure of himself. "Trust me."

She held her breath and lowered her head, then clasped Carl's hand tightly. He turned on the flashlight on his phone and led the way without hesitation. A few seconds later, they reached the beach, and Kris let out a tense, long breath.

The light of the waning gibbous Moon reflected against the calm ocean waves, sending flickers of light everywhere and covering the beach in silver shadows. They were completely alone. The only creatures keeping them company were pale crabs that took bellicose stances when Kris and Carl stomped the sand around them, giggling.

"See? Told you," Carl said, "no one's going to see us out here. We can do whatever we want," he said playfully.

Kris squealed and ran toward the lifeguard tower. In daylight, the tower showed its bright yellow and orange, a splash of joyful colors on the tourist-abundant stretch of sand. At night, the structure appeared gloomy, resembling a menacing creature on tall, insect-like legs.

"It looks like one of those aliens from *War of the Worlds*," Kris said, then promptly started running, waving her arms up in the air, pretending she was flying.

Carl chased Kris, laughing and squealing with her, running in circles around the tower, and weaving footstep patterns between the solid wood posts.

"Phew," Carl said, stopping his chase and taking some distance. "Stinks of piss. Let's get out of here."

"Eww…" Kris replied, following him. "Why do men do that?"

"What? Pee?"

"Everybody pees, genius," Kris replied, still panting from the run. "Peeing where it stinks and bothers people, that's what I meant. Women pee in the bushes. Men should pee in the water if they don't like the bushes."

"Really? That's gross."

"Where do you think fish pee? At least the waves would wash away the pee and it wouldn't stink, to mess up our sunrise."

"Fish pee?" Carl pushed back, incredulous.

"They don't?"

They walked holding hands, putting a few more yards of distance between them and the tower. Then Carl suddenly dropped to the ground, dragging Kris with him. She squealed again, and laughed.

"Let's sit here," he said. "The show's on. Let's see if we get a good one."

The sky was starting to light up toward the east. They watched silently, hand in hand, as the dark shades of blue and gray gradually turned ablaze, mixing in dark reds and orange hues. The horizon line was clear, a sharp edge marking where ocean met sky.

"It's going to be great," Carl said. "No clouds, no haze." He kissed her lips quickly, and then turned his attention back to the celestial light show.

"You're a strange boy, Carl."

"Yeah? Why?"

"Other boys would have asked me to sneak out in the middle of the night to make out. With you, it's a sunrise, period. Should I worry?"

Carl smiled widely, then tickled Kris until she begged for mercy between gasps of air and bouts of uncontrollable laughter.

"Stop! Stop it already. I can't breathe!"

"I might want to get on with that make out, you know," Carl laughed.

"Nah, it's getting light. Someone could see us," Kris pushed back, unconvinced. "Someone could come by."

Carl shrugged and turned his attention to the sunrise. He grabbed her hand and held it gently, playing with her fingers.

Almost half the sky had caught fire, challenging the moonlight, and obliterating most of its reflected light against the blissful, serene, ocean waves.

Carl checked the time on his phone.

"A few more minutes until it comes out," he announced, sounding serious, as if predicting a rare and significant event. He took a few pictures of the sky, then suddenly snapped one of Kris.

"Ah... no," she reacted, "give that to me right this second, Carl." She grabbed the phone from his hand and looked at the picture he'd taken. The image showed a young girl with messy, golden brown hair, partially covering a scrunched, tense face with deep ridges on her brow. The snapshot revealed Kris biting her index fingernail, totally absorbed by the process, slobbering her sleeve cuff while at it.

"God-awful," she reacted, then pressed the option to delete.

"No!" Carl said, pulling the phone from her hands. "I like it!"

"There's nothing to like. There," she said, relaxing a little, and arranging her hair briefly with her long, thin fingers. "I'll pose for you." She smiled.

Carl took a few pictures. She looked gorgeous, against the backdrop of fiery skies, pink sand, and turquoise water. He took image after image, as she got into it and made faces, danced, and swirled in front of him, laughing.

The sun's first piercing ray shot out of the sea, just as Kris shrieked, a blood-curdling scream that got Carl to spring to his feet and run to her.

Speechless, Kris pointed a trembling hand at the lifeguard tower. Underneath the tower, between the wooden posts supporting the elevated structure, was the naked body of a young woman. She appeared to be kneeling, as if praying to the rising sun. Her hands were clasped together in front of her in the universal, unmistakable gesture of silent pleading.

Holding their breaths, they approached carefully, curious and yet afraid of what they stood to discover. The growing light of the new morning revealed more details with each step they took. Her back, covered in bruises and small cuts, stained in smudged, dried blood. Her blue eyes wide open, glossed over. A few specks of sand clung to her long, dark lashes. Her beautiful face, immobile, covered in sparkling flecks of sand. Her lips slightly parted, as if to let a last breath escape. Long, blonde hair, wet from sea spray, almost managed to disguise the deep cut in her neck.

No blood dripped from the wound; her heart had stopped beating for some time. Yet she held upright, unyielding in her praying posture, her knees stuck firmly in the sand covered in their footprints, and her eyes fixed on the beautiful sunrise they came to enjoy.

~~~*End Preview*~~~

Like *Dawn Girl*?

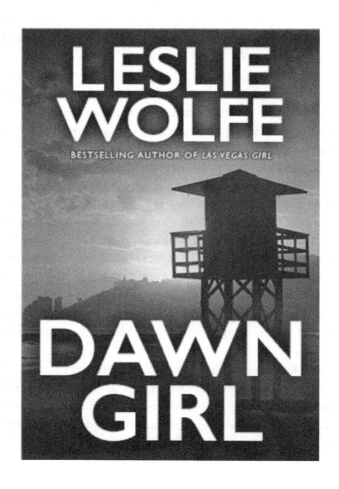

Buy It now!

About the Author

Leslie Wolfe is a bestselling author whose novels break the mold of traditional thrillers. She creates unforgettable, brilliant, strong women heroes who deliver fast-paced, satisfying suspense, backed up by extensive background research in technology and psychology.

Leslie released the first novel, *Executive,* in October 2011. Since then, she has written many more, continuing to break down barriers of traditional thrillers. Her style of fast-paced suspense, backed up by extensive background research in technology and psychology, has made Leslie one of the most read authors in the genre and she has created an array of unforgettable, brilliant and strong women heroes along the way.

Reminiscent of the television drama *Criminal Minds,* her series of books featuring the fierce and relentless FBI Agent **Tess Winnett** would be of great interest to readers of James Patterson, Melinda Leigh, and David Baldacci crime thrillers. Fans of Kendra Elliot and Robert Dugoni suspenseful mysteries would love the **Las Vegas Crime** series, featuring the tension-filled relationship between Baxter and Holt. Finally, her **Alex Hoffmann** series of political and espionage action adventure will enthrall readers of Tom Clancy, Brad Thor, and Lee Child.

Leslie has received much acclaim for her work, including inquiries from Hollywood, and her books offer something that is different and tangible, with readers becoming invested in not only the main characters and plot but also with the ruthless minds of the killers she creates.

A complete list of Leslie's titles is available at LeslieWolfe.com/books.

Leslie enjoys engaging with readers every day and would love to hear from you. Become an insider: gain early access to previews of Leslie's new novels.

- Email: LW@WolfeNovels.com
- Facebook: https://www.facebook.com/wolfenovels
- Follow Leslie on Amazon: http://bit.ly/WolfeAuthor
- Follow Leslie on BookBub: http://bit.ly/wolfebb
- Website: www.LeslieWolfe.com
- Visit Leslie's Amazon store: http://bit.ly/WolfeAll

Made in United States
North Haven, CT
06 August 2023

39999865R00161